The Passionate Mistakes
and Intricate Corruption of One
Girl in America

The Passionate Mistakes and Intricate Corruption of One Girl in America

Michelle Tea

Semiotext(e) / Smart Art Press

New York   Santa Monica

Thank yous to the Bearded Lady, Jenny Joseph, Kris
Kovick, Miriam Kronberg and Bucky Sinster; to Sini
Anderson, Cari Campbell, Ali Liebegott, Malaina Jean
Poore, Sparrow 13 and David West; to Cathy DuBois,
Renee Brunk, and Guen Colvin wherever she is; to Chris
Kraus, Susan Martin, and Eileen Myles; and to everyone in
San Francisco ThankyouThankyouThankyou

This is Smart Art Press Volume IV, No. 37

ISBN: 1-57027-074-0

Semiotext(e)   Smart Art Press
Editorial Office: Bergamot Station
522 Philosophy Hall   2525 Michigan Avenue
Columbia University   Building C-1
New York, NY 10027   Santa Monica, CA 90404

                                 Tel: 310.264.4678
semiotexte@aol.com   Fax: 310.264.4682
                                 www.smartartpress.com

Book design by Ben Meyers

We gratefully acknowledge financial assistance in the
publication of this book from the Literature Program of
the New York State Council on the Arts.

Printed in the United States of America

10 9 8 7 6 5 4 3 2

For
Kathleen Phyllis
and
Peter Anthony

We, amnesiacs all, condemned to live in an eternally fleeting present, have created the most elaborate of human constructions, memory, to buffer ourselves against the intolerable knowledge of the irreversible passage of time and irretrievability of its moments and events.

—Geoffrey Sonnabend

I was in front of the Orpheum Theater in Boston, watching INXS climb out of their tour bus. I was fourteen years old and this was a very exciting moment for me. There was a split second when the tour bus seemed to quiver and all the girls in black clothes became hushed, clove cigarettes halted, and the door swung open and in the shining frame of the bus was the band, moving out of the darkness. And then a pause like an intake of breath and the girls just descended upon them and everything split open. They were locusts, they enveloped the band and of course everyone wanted the singer. Girls were harvesting curls from his head, grabbing his denim jacket, screaming. The rest of the band may as well have been roadies, they were so ignored. And of course I wanted to touch the singer too, it's why I had been there for hours smoking Marlboro Lights in front of the glitzy tour bus, waiting. But I just could not toss myself into the context of those girls. I leaned against a building and smoked. This had always been my curse in my desire to be a groupie, my refusal to become part of the shrieking mob. I mean, how embarrassing. It did make a case for female hysteria. There was crying and there was moaning, girls hopping up and down, girls with gifts and album covers and autograph books, art school girls with charcoal portraits of the corkscrew-curled singer. I wanted to meet these musicians as equals, be their friend, have a conversation so they could see how cool and deep I was. I was leaning into the brick of a building, smoking, probably I looked removed and superior; distant hence mysterious. I had realized my catholic school skirt was the punkest thing I owned so I was wearing it, the hem ripped off and tied into my hair, anarchy symbols penned into the plaid. I was playing hard to get with the singer. Instead the saxophone player took notice and came my way, this tall and skinny weird looking guy. I was wearing a necklace, pink plastic pearls with a dangling silver cross. His hand swooped toward it, moving smoothly up and over my left tit. *That's a great necklace* he said. Please. Even I knew it was a cheap piece of trash, I got it at the mall for, what, two dollars. This guy from INXS had totally felt me up. You know which one he is, he's wearing socks with British flags on them in that video, he's on the floor playing his saxophone and his pants ride up and you see the socks. The one with the glasses. At that tender moment in my adolescence I had nary a chest to speak of. You really had to go out of your way to bump into it. I was flattered and repulsed. If it had been the singer it might've been different. Thanks I said, and quickly moved away from the lecherous rock star.

That's when I met Judith and Janet. At first you couldn't tell they were twins. They really played it down, Janet keeping her hair short and shaved and kind of red, and Judith going for the Siouxsie look, big and black with bangs long enough to hide the face she shared with her sister. Judith and Janet took an immediate liking to me, very swiftly a relationship developed that was practically romantic. They were buying me things — food, cigarettes, gifts. A heart-shaped plastic pin that said

Rebel. A black beret like the one worn by the drummer for INXS. It was like they were courting me. We would go into Boston together, Boston at this point still being new and exciting, the Big City. Judith and Janet were very into the Smiths and Morrissey and were therefore vegetarians and it was really amusing to go to McDonalds with them and watch them order meatless hamburgers. The girl taking their order had this defensive hesitation, like were they fucking with her or what, and Judith would get all intense about the french fries being cooked in vegetable oil. They were so weird. Who cared. I was eating a Big Mac and they'd be looking faint and revolted, nibbling on ketchup-soaked buns. Judith and Janet's parents were divorced and they lived with their father which was strange and it got even stranger when you went to their home and watched them interact. It was crazy. Their father was dangerous, you knew that immediately and tried to stay out of his way but it was hard because he was doing this hey-I'm-a-cool-dad thing and he'd want to hang out and kid with you but his jokes were often mean and creepy. Like he had some sleazy personal ad, probably an escort ad because the headline was a name and the name was Michelle and he went on to read me the woman's measurements and the carefully coded description of what she was offering. *Is that you, Michelle?* He looked at my chest and smirked. Another time I was wearing this cute little retro dress, black with a veil of chiffon hanging from the collar, and he grabbed the chiffon part, held it in his hand like a shadow, said *What's this* and just tore it from the dress. And there was *Hey don't spill your drink* as he whacked the cup so apple juice went splashing down my t-shirt.

He was this disgusting red-haired man and I remember him most clearly in his bathrobe. He sold drugs, that's how he made his money. That and betting on greyhounds. Apparently he did quite well because he had this really fancy car that talked. Like if you left the door unlocked this spooky computer voice would say *passenger door is unlocked.* He'd leave the doors unlocked on purpose to impress us with this luxury and to be honest I was impressed. Judith and Janet were not. They really hated their father, it was a bonding point for us because I hated my father too and we would talk about getting them in a room together and blowing it up. Judith and Janet were very upfront about how they hated their father, right to his face, and it was unbelievable to witness such brutal honesty between child and parent. I could never tell my father to fuck off.

The father had a separate phone line from Judith and Janet, I guess it was his business phone. We'd be hanging out in their bedroom listening to records and planning our next hair styles and the phone would ring and it would be him, calling from his bedroom right next door. *Make your own fucking tuna fish sandwich daddy!* Judith screamed and slammed down the phone. It was really incredible. He wasn't like a father, he was like a scuzzy guy you had to put up with, like some freak on the bus who you'd tell to fuck off but he was their father and they had to live with him, telling him to fuck off over and over. Once he went away for a while and left Judith and Janet all this money plus a gallon of vodka and some pot. I stopped trying to understand their relationship at that point. I just drank the vodka and was glad he was gone. I was at their house so often it was

12

like he was my father too. Once I went to their mom's house for dinner. I was nervous. I mean, if their father was the more fit parent, what was their mom like? She was like Stevie Nicks. Blonde, kind of mystical-looking. She lived by herself in this cute little apartment. We ate matzoh ball soup and homemade brownies. It was actually spookier to find her so pleasant and normal. She just didn't want kids so Judith and Janet ended up with their father. But how could she do that. Surely she knew what he was like. One night, I can't remember what happened but it ended with Judith in the kitchen shrieking, throwing glass plate after glass plate to shatter on the linoleum, and her father was just laughing and telling her to clean it up. Judith and Janet both cut their arms, they had all these scars, one in the shape of a pentacle on Judith's left shoulder. It just seemed like an accessory to me, like the black clothes and pointy english boots, kind of pretentious and dumb.

Me and Judith and Janet would be friends for so long and then we wouldn't be. I never understood why. They just adored you for so long then wham! they hated you. We had three separate eras of friendship, the first being when I was fourteen and didn't know anyone. Then later, I was hanging around with the death-rock-slash-skater crowd in Boston and they turned up and everyone was like *oh those are the Cure girls, they're crazy.* They were crazy. They would come and sit together away from everyone and slice their arms and write furiously in their journals. Before long we were friends again. Their father said they could have a party for Halloween and I helped them put it together. It was a huge production. Judith was dressing up like a lesbian

13

dominatrix so we made the bedroom a dungeon, with big heavy chains and black streamers hanging from the ceiling. Another room we covered with trash bags and plugged in tv sets set on static, that was the room for the kids who were on drugs. I dressed up like Cleopatra and carried grapes around with me. I have a photo from that night, a black wig and eye makeup dipping green grapes into my mouth. It was taken right before I puked and blacked out. The party was a disaster. I had invited all these speed metal kids from the vocational high school I went to and the father saw them coming in with cases of beer and freaked out. I guess it was only ok if he bought it for us. One of the metalheads, Dez, raped the pumpkin girl in the backyard. She was a girl from Janet's school who came in a pumpkin costume, she left crying and screaming and the party became divided by those who believed her and those who believed Dez, who said nothing happened. I had by then passed out in the trash bag room and missed the whole thing. Judith and Janet soon hated me again, a mysterious animosity continuing for about a year. I think it was '88 and they loved me again. It was summer, I was riding the subway with Judith one night and the conductor's seat at the rear of the train was unlocked and vacant. We were completely wrecked off vodka and Veryfine juice, sitting in the conductor's seat watching the spooky dark tunnel zoom by. I was saying Why Do We Always End Up Hating Each Other but what I meant was Why Do You Always End Up Hating Me? Judith was saying *I don't know I don't know* and we swore it would never happen again. I liked her so much right then. That was the year she went glamorous. She got a nose job. Insurance covered it because she convinced a psychologist that her regular bumpy nose caused her emotional pain. She got a new little button nose that was not nearly as cool as her old kitchen witch nose. She bleached her hair blonde, slicked it back and started going out with Chris Busk, which was weird. He had been my boyfriend for a week but I dumped him because he was really a thief and couldn't be trusted. Me and Judith had this thing with Chris, we pretended we were having a lesbian affair to make him jealous. Me and Judith in front of the Boston Public Library holding our jackets over our faces and moving our heads like we were kissing. Our faces were so close we may as well have just done it. One weekend my parents went away, a rare occurrence, and I had some people over and me and Judith had this very elaborate plan to go into my room and moan loudly until Chris came in and found us embracing in our underwear. It never happened. They ended up having sex in my bed while I slept in my parents room and cried about this fag Jose who everyone had a crush on that summer. We kept the fake affair going for a while because it was fun to watch Chris get jealous and sulk. I couldn't stand him. And then Judith and Janet hated me again and that was that. I never even saw them again, they just disappeared. Someone bumped into Janet a few years ago at the library, she was going to college and had a Brazilian boyfriend. Judith was always crazier so naturally her story is more intense. She got some trashy boyfriend who sold cocaine and eventually he got busted and narced on everyone to stay out of jail. He and Judith are in the witness relocation plan, living somewhere in California under different identities. And I know I wouldn't know her if I saw her.

Goth-n-Roll High School
Boston, 1987

At the back of this nightclub called the Channel was a wooden pier that sat squatly over the Charles river and that's where the guys were taking this woman. They were metalhead guys, really Kenmore Square with their long flyaway hair and fringed everything. All I could see of the woman was her ass, wrapped in a bit of black leather and slung over the shoulder of the tallest guy. She was wearing one of those skirts I wanted so badly but couldn't afford, a leather miniskirt, the sides pinned together with skull buckles. She wasn't wearing any underwear, you could tell when she kicked her legs and she kicked her legs a lot, batted the guy on the chest screaming *put me down* and laughing, a shrill sound that got lost inside the deeper laughter of the guys who carried her around to the back of the nightclub, gone. I had spent the earlier part of the evening inside my bedroom with the nailpolish graffiti marking up the cracked linoleum, with the tinseled windowshades and mutilated Barbie knick knacks. In front of the long mirror affixed to the aluminum wardrobe that held my clothes, taking my hair in thick black chunks and raking the comb through it backwards, blasting it with some Extra Super Hold, and watching it slowly fall back onto my head, hopeless. My mother was clucking in the doorway, a cigarette in hand, Vantage, the ones with the gross little tunnel in the filter that you can watch turn yellower and yellower as you smoke, like

16

lungs. She still had her white nurse uniform on, the pin with her name, the soft white shoes. She blew smoke into my room and bit her lip. *You got such nice hair* she clucked, watching my desperate attempts to destroy it. It was an extra special night, the Lords of the New Church were playing at that club in Boston, the one by the water. I was fifteen and too young to actually go to the show, but I figured I could maybe meet them. I didn't meet them. I met Joez, while the Lords played loud inside, and outside, in the parking lot, gloomy teenagers chain-smoked and glared at each other. I was with my friend Tracey, we were in our shaky beginners makeup. Some boy who had Nina Hagen and a bunch of spaceships on the back of his jacket called us poseurs and smoked sulky cigarettes. There was long haired Laura with the bolero hat, and Joez, who had the most perfect mask of makeup I'd ever seen. Her eyeliner slunk from the corners of her eyes, tapering into sharp little points. She wore impressive lipliner, shaping her mouth into two red peaks, and her eyebrows arched thinly. Joez's makeup was sharp and deadly on her soft round face. She wore a perfect coat of white on her skin, like a slipcover over good furniture. In the dark Channel parking lot she held a dusty compact in her palm and patted the powder all over her face, slid red lipstick over her lips. Joez was beautiful. He hair was big when I met her and like her melancholy it swelled with time, starting out thick red and clumpy, held back with black lace, and by the time she hated me it was longer and brown, the clumps welded solid by her ritual of Aqua Net and a crimping iron. Soak the long tangles in hairspray and feed it to the hot teeth of the iron, the silver zig-zag sizzling. You could actually hear Joez destroying

17

her hair. Then more hair spray and the skinny teasing comb that looked like an ice pick. Joez had it down. She lived in Salem so she was quite authentic in her black cloth and glinting metal spiderwebs. She was very sarcastic about the Salem pseudo-witch culture that me and my Boston friends loved. There was that woman Laurie Cabot, the Official Witch of Salem, she had a book and a shop and blessed the Salem High football team in her long black cape. The media loved her each October, she'd be on talk shows and in the Boston Globe explaining how Halloween was a holy day for her. Laurie Cabot drove a spooky black car and almost ran Joez over in it once, earning her the nickname The Official Bitch of Salem. Joez said Laurie Cabot's little witch shop was for dumb tourists who wanted love potions and voodoo dolls and ugly satin jackets with flashy pentacles silkscreened on the back. Joez knew where the real witches shopped, wooden places with shelves of glass jars and an earthy smell. Joez was smart. Almost right away she was my best friend, though at first there was that really bad boyfriend she had, Rox. He wanted to be Jim Morrison and he did in fact resemble the lizard king. He needed leather pants. I thought he was a dork and I told Joez so. I'd see them shopping together in Harvard Square, all in black with those round pilgrimy hats on their heads. Rox would tense up when anyone talked to Joez, you could tell he didn't want her to have any friends. One night they came to the library steps where everyone hung out and drank vodka. The library was in Copley Square, and the scene there was a real mishmash. Mostly everyone was some form of death rock or goth, but there were skaters too, and sleek-looking artsy girls. Everyone was young, in high school, and some of the skater boys weren't even that old. Tyler and Kenny had to be about 12. They were adorable, they were our mascots and all the girls would coo maternally at them. They called me ID Lady because I had found some girl's drivers license at a Siouxsie show and used it to buy everyone liquor. It was really perfect because the girl in the picture had fucked up purple hair and all this makeup, so you really didn't know what she looked like. The guys at the liquor store would just shrug and bag up my order. I collected everyone's money, I'd have to write it all down the orders were so long: vodka, rum, 40 ouncers for the boys, sometimes a six pack, wine coolers and there was that time I turned everyone on to Manischewitz, Jewish table wine that tasted like zyrex and was only two dollars a bottle. Usually there would be money left over, as much as 10 or 20 dollars, and I kept it as a tip. It was like a job. Basically, everyone would just stand around and get really drunk, smoke lots of cigarettes, some of the more disturbed gothic girls would start to cry and maybe cut up their arms. It was a phenomenon I didn't understand but it was very popular. Lots of girls had scars going up their forearm and down their shoulder, they wore them like proud tattoos. I thought it was dumb. Sometimes kids would puke or cops would come and tell us to move. We peed inside this incredibly ornate hotel near the library, chandeliers and great persian rugs. We'd be totally wrecked with tangled hair and black lipstick, scaring the wealthy. We stole flowers from the vases in the ladies room, and on the way out swiped a glass bowl of peanuts from the bar.

When Joez first started coming to Copley she always had stupid Rox on her arm, that hat like a big black dinner plate hiding his disappearing hairline. Rox would climb up onto one of the moldy-looking statues at the front of the library, and perch there like a gargoyle, watching Joez, looking down his skinny nose at all the drunk and hyper kids. Me and Joez stumbled past, our arms looped around each other's waists. *I bet she wouldn't like you if she knew...* he called down at Joez. *Knew what?* she yelled. *About you and Monica* he taunted. I Know About Her And Monica I shot at him and pulled Joez away. Joez made out with a girl once, her friend Monica who was so goth and quiet and cool you thought she was on drugs. Monica actually slept with Stiv Bators the last time the Lords of the New Church were in town. Joez told me how Monica's mother was banging on the hotel room door while Joez and Monica hid in the bathroom and Stiv searched the floor for his pants. Joez had exciting stories. Not so much things she had done, it was more the wild behavior of others that pulled her along and I thought maybe she thought I was also wild and felt inspired to bring her adventures. Joez had quit high school, got her GED and enrolled in poetry courses at a community college. She just hit fast forward and skipped right over the segment of life I was currently mired in, attending my vocational high school, miserably asleep at my computer. The teachers didn't care if we lived or died. I hung out in the bathroom smoking and explaining my hairdo to the other smoking girls with their awful just-outside-Boston accents. Acted crazy in the hallways so the boys would leave me alone. Tried to write sad poetry in math class and the teacher would hurl dusty erasers at me leaving big chalk marks on my black lace dresses. Joez's poems were better than mine. Her pen name was Phiend, the second half of her full name Joe-sephine, though her parents called her Jennifer or even worse Jenny. It made her crazy. Joez had exceptionally bad parents. Her mother was a tight fake woman with a shrill voice. She had grown up really poor and never stopped telling Joez how good she had it, how she had walked through the cold New England winters with barely a jacket to keep the wind off. She seemed deter-mined to make Joez relive her experience. Joez wore pointy death rock boots wrapped in electrical tape because she couldn't ask for a new pair without hearing about how her mom never had new shoes when she was growing up. Joez would take the commuter rail into Boston each weekend with a twenty-dollar bill in the square snapped pocket of her leather jacket. She would be terrified to break the twenty and do this annoying trick where she would ask you to buy all these little things for her, subway tokens and cans of Jolt, because she didn't want to break her bill. By the time the weekend was up you would've spent six or seven dollars on her. Joez never worked. I always had some crappy job, conve-nience stores, copy shops, hair salons. Joez worked maybe a week at a supermarket and that was it. It was hard because Salem is a small town and she looked like such a freak with her spider hair and exquisite makeup. Later when we hated each other I heard she got a job at the witchcraft store she made fun of, but while we were friends she just took her poetry classes and rode the train in each weekend with her twenty-dollar bill and a con-tainer of guar gum, this powder she mixed with water so she wouldn't have to eat. Joez spent her twenty on vodka and wine and if there was enough left over, records.

Joez's favorite was Sisters of Mercy and mine was Christian Death and we both loved Siouxsie, the Cure, Lords of the New Church, the Mission U.K., Bauhaus.

This is how the weekend worked: I would ride the bus into Boston on Friday night, alone with my book on my lap and all my weird makeup, black hair and black lipstick, and hopefully the bus riders of Chelsea Massachusetts would leave me alone but usually I would have to endure some kind of humiliation that only strengthened my idea of myself as a beautiful and noble martyr. I had gone to Catholic School and I understood that the most special and most perfect were always persecuted, I would sit in my collar and my black lace dress and gaze out the window as we passed over the choppy harbor. And Joez would be there on the other side of the bridge, holding a plastic Tower Records bag packed with clothes for the weekend, books, a walkman for the train. She'd ditched Rox, that drag, it had taken forever and he had all but stalked her but he was gone now, and Joez was mine. If it was really terrible weather like snow or rain we would climb down into Haymarket Station and take the green line, but it was best when we walked. Climbing the slowly rising steps at Government Center where boring normal people ate lunch during the week but at night it was big and empty like a swimming pool with all the water drained out. We'd walk downtown where it was busier and more exciting, people darting around beneath the streetlights. We were walking into a great drunken adventure. Past the rat-ridden alley that led to the Orpheum Theater where bands we liked often played. Joez saw the Cure there which was amazing because now they were so huge they only played enormous alienating places where it was impossible to jump on stage or meet them. Down the street from the Orpheum was a teeny little liquor store that sold 2 for 1 bottles of wine and I would grab a couple by their slender necks, the dark red sloshing around inside, and we would walk across the street to the Boston Common and start our journey through the winding path that always looked different depending on the season. If it was white and icy and the ugly naked trees were hung with lights we would take quick little steps, hurried in the cold but careful not to slip. Maybe duck into the underground garage and drink our drinks there, but only if it was really freezing. If it was autumn we would kick through crunchy leaves, and summer was best, the most perfect slow stroll beneath trees that had leaves on, us maybe bare shouldered but probably not because part of the gothic aesthetic was keeping yourself covered. In humid Boston summers it was hard, sweating under black sleeves and tights, makeup melting, hair collapsing damply on your head. But summer nights were perfect when we would cross the street into the Public Gardens, nicer than the Common with empty fountains and rows of flowers and the shallow pond where the swan boats sat tethered and sleeping. We'd go beneath the bridge to the pier where in the daylight lines of tourists twist and sweat, waiting for a ride in a big floating swan. At night it was just me and Joez and bunches of spiders that spun webs all over the wood of the pier, you had to be careful not to lean your head back into one. Me and Joez liked them, they were the pets of this our little clubhouse where we would pull the corks from our bottles and drink. Don't ask me what we talked about but we never shut up. Lots of laughing. We were death rock but we weren't depressed, though Joez did have her moments and there were more and more as time progressed. I would smoke, Marlboro Lights, and Joez wouldn't. The more I drank the more I smoked the more I talked. The more I drank the more I fell in love. With everything. The scuzzy pond beneath us, the buildings twinkling beyond the trees, cars zooming by somewhere. And all of my life would just swell up inside me and soon I'd have to pee. So we'd leave our little pier, legs cramped and drunker when we stood. Leave the park and be on Newbury Street in front of the Ritz-Carlton. Push through the revolving door and glide across the marble floor like we were supposed to be there, hotel people giving us awful looks. If they kicked us out we'd go back to the park and pee under a tree or in an empty fountain, but normally we would walk proudly down the carpeted stairs and pee in the tasteful white bathroom of the Ritz-Carlton. No paper anything, they had plush facecloths and fluffy towels and a wicker hamper to toss them in when you were finished primping. Joez would fix her makeup in the long lit mirror. I would tease my hair, give it a spray, maybe put on some of Joez's lipstick. My eyeliner was always thicker than hers, like I used a crayon and she used some sort of elegant paintbrush. We would leave the bathroom a mess and I would always steal something completely useless like a bottle of softsoap or a towel. Things I would inevitably forget on a sidewalk later, when I was drunker. Being in that placid white bathroom just made me want to destroy. I took the plant that sat on the sink and tore the thick green leaves from its vine, threw them all over the floor. Stomped on them til they left smudges of green plant blood on the floor, me and Joez laughing. She thought it was mean but she didn't stop me. She stuffed her Tower Records bag with facecloths and we left.

After ruining the bathroom at the Ritz-Carlton me and Joez would stroll up Newbury Street, a street that starts out old and wealthy with fur shops and Shreves, and grows gradually hipper and wealthier with haute couture shops and millions of hair salons. We'd have our bottles, Joez and I, if not wine then juice and 100 proof blue label Smirnoff, though Joez did like to mix hers with Jolt, a cocktail affectionately called Brown Vodka. So strong it stung the raw windburned skin of my lips. Joez laughed at my cringe and said *mother's milk*. Me and Joez would hold hands and be so obnoxious because glassy rich Newbury Street was not us, the fawning window shoppers weren't weird like us and it made us yell and sing loud and laugh at how normal and dumb everything was. And as we turned onto Boyleston Street where the fat grey library sat the feeling of entering something would overwhelm me, like the first chords of your favorite song but we were the song, moving through the street to the place where all the kids were. Skater boys jerking around on their boards, clean girls with dyed hair huddled together over their bottles. Sometimes real punks like the crew of mohawked homeless kids from Orange County, a place we all knew from Suburbia. We all felt fake around them. And then what would happen. Everyone was drunk, running around. Someone would know about a party and we'd go, someone would have acid and a real adventure would begin. A cop would tell us to move and we'd walk down to the river. Or we'd hang out on the library stairs all night, peeing in the alleys behind the building, helping the ones who got too drunk and puked or started crying. I did that once, after my grandmother died. It was actually a good six months after her death and I realized I hadn't done anything meaningful to say goodbye to her, and I started bawling and burping and carrying on to this boy PJ about how I had to bury an amethyst in the ground beneath my grandmother's headstone because she had been an aquarius, like me. PJ and his boyfriend Jimy were the only out queers and we called them the Gay Punks. PJ was tall thin and pockmarked with bright red hair and he did a lot of acid. He and Jimy would drink too much and have fist fights that ended up with PJ crying and Jimy storming off. PJ used my weepy outburst as a channel to express his own misery and we sat hugging and sobbing until I got up and barfed. I remember a girl named Mercy who I didn't really like took care of me, got me into Peter's car where I sat on someone's lap and puked out the window. They were all going to *Rocky Horror* and I had been so excited to go that I drank too much and ultimately passed out, was deposited at Tracey's house, carried onto the couch and whoever took off my boots must have lost all patience with me because the laces were busted. My favorite necklace was somehow broken. I woke in the morning so hungover, with no idea where I was. A little scratchy noise woke me and I found Tracey scrubbing a puddle of bile I'd thrown up in my sleep from the carpet. *That's how Jimi Hendrix died* she told me. Everyone had had the best time at *Rocky Horror* and I was sad. At that time *Rocky Horror* was the big thing to do each weekend, the Friday and the Saturday shows at the little cinema in Harvard Square. We were groupies, we knew all the things you yell at the screen, we were friends with the cast of the floor show. James who

26

did Columbia was my first drag queen friend. He would go down to the Greyhound terminal where all the young boys leaned against buildings waiting for tricks, but James would mug his. He and his boyfriend would beat the guy up and steal his wallet. James told me if he ever got AIDS he would take as many people with him as possible. James, I said. He did an OK Columbia. I was dying to be Columbia, but I wasn't really allowed to go to *Rocky Horror*. I had to lie and say I was at other people's houses. For a little while I had a boyfriend, Percy, who wanted to be Frankenfurter. Percy cultivated an evil persona and everyone said he did black magic so I got a crush on him. I was with him in the empty theater and he was acting seductive like a vampire. *Are you scared of me* he asked and I wasn't but I said Yes because I wanted to be. Percy wore a black cape, he fingered my dog collar and said *I'll put velvet on this so it won't chafe your neck*. Percy was such a fag. We'd make out and I'd go home with his red lipstick smudged on my face and my mother would be really tense. Once we were together in the trunk of Peter's car and I gave him a hickey and experimented briefly with his dick and my mouth. I heard from my friends that he didn't really enjoy it. Percy got to be Frankenfurter one night when the regular Frank was out of town. He was so excited. I brought him a bouquet of baby blue balloons tied with shiny ribbons. He was magnificent. The outfit, the makeup, the perfect cruel pout, the curl of his mouth when he sneered. I had been thinking about breaking up with him but when I saw him like that, all tough in his corset, I swooned. When on the big screen Frankenfurter dies, plummeting from the radio tower, Percy hurled himself off a chair, hitting the floor with a thud and a scream. It was spectacular. I sat in the front row with Joez, whose big white face made her Magenta, and we clutched each other and cheered at the passionate demise of our painted hero.

Sometimes the skinheads would come around. We knew about the skinheads before the news show on Channel 5 did a piece on them and before the big article in the *Boston Globe* that listed their nazi bootlace code, similar to the fag hanky code but entirely different. We knew that white meant white power, but red meaning beat 'em til they're red and bloody was a new color to scan for. The legend was that the skinheads had come down from Rhode Island, a whole gang of them. The photo in the Boston Globe showed them posed menacingly before a huge swastika tapestry in some dingy apartment, probably Allston. I half-recognized them. It was hard because you tried not to look at them when they came by and also because they were so identical in their uniform round white heads and puffy jackets. The hairdos on the girls were baffling, shorn save for a bleach blonde fringe that circled their scalp. Really unattractive. It was so they looked fearsome like the boys but still retained some femininity. Stormy was the scariest. She had a baby, you'd see her pushing the stroller, surrounded by her gang of thugs. The rumor was that the baby had an american flag tattooed on its arm, but no one could get close enough to verify. You should understand the different neighborhoods of Boston counterculture in the 80s. There was Harvard Square which, while it did have a family of hippies wandering around in their ratty layers, was really for punks. I mean real punks. These kids had safety pins in their faces and really filthy clothing and I think many of them didn't have homes. They were authentic. I was kind of scared of them, particularly the girls, who looked incredibly tough. I had a job in Harvard Square, handing out coupon books on the street. One of the annoying people in red shirts attempting to hand-deliver you some junk mail. The coupon books were called The Square Deal and I would stand on a corner with my arm outstretched barking Square Deal, Square Deal, mortified at how low I had sunk. I would see people I knew on their way to their real jobs at boutiques and record stores. One day I was assigned to the part of Harvard Square known as The Pit. It was a wide depression in the middle of the sidewalk with concrete benches and a slope for skateboarding, and it was there that the punks hung out. I was terrified. What a dorky job, I was sure they were going to hassle me, maybe even beat me up. A blonde girl, short with a nose ring, came up and asked me how much I got paid. I got paid by the book, so much for each one handed out. *Why don't you just throw them out* she asked, jerking her head towards the trashcan. But I had been warned about the Square Deal spies that cruised by your post and peeked into trashcans to make sure you weren't cheating. *We can take a bunch and dump them in the river for you* she said. I couldn't believe it. I am always so astounded by niceness. These kids must have been really bored. It was the girl and a couple of equally scruffy punk boys, they hefted up my stack of Square Deals and hauled them down to the Charles River. I gave them some cigarettes. A week or so later I lied to my job and said my aunt died because I'm really wimpy about just quitting a job. The Square Deal people were really sad, they said I was one of their best workers.

The kids that hung out in Kenmore Square were older, out of school, and a lot of them played in bands. They didn't look punk but they were really into the music. They looked like jocks actually, the boys did. They looked like boys who would beat you up for looking weird and some of them did. I have never understood this little subculture of frat boys into hardcore but it does exist. There were always fights in Kenmore Square. The boys from New Kids On The Block hung out there before they got so disgustingly famous. One night I was hanging out with some of the jocky hardcore boys, I was drunk and we were spare-changing for beer money. This little terror on a skateboard named Damian was chanting *get the punks drunk, get the punks drunk* to the throngs of normal people leaving the Red Sox game. The boys I was with were starting a band and I was telling them how I was learning to play bass and they thought maybe I could wear a skimpy leather outfit and play with them. One boy lifted me up and started carrying me around, he was drunk too, everyone in Kenmore Square was usually drunk, and all of a sudden one of the boys from New Kids on the Block was there grabbing my ass. It was Danny, the one that looks like an ape. I kicked him in the shoulder. This was before everyone knew who they were. Later, when they were on MTV my boyfriend bumped into him at a club and embarked upon a retroactive defense of my soiled honor. *My girlfriend said you grabbed her ass once,* he said. As if he would remember. I'm sure he grabbed asses all the time, those boys are such pricks. *I don't grab a girl's ass,* said the superstar, *I FEEL a girl's ass. But tell her I'm sorry.* Thanks, Danny.

The death rockers of Copley were hated by all the other Boston subcultures. The punks thought we were silly and pretentious and came from rich families, and the hardcore boys thought all of our boys were fags and they were probably right. The martyrs this made of us was a good fashion accessory, but it sucked to have no allies when the skinheads started coming around. First they were just kind of intimidating, they'd huddle in a group a few feet away and mock us, whisper and laugh and yell things like *what the fuck are you looking at* when the truth was we avoided eye contact with the skinheads like we avoided sunlight. Once Stormy was there and the baby was out of the stroller, crawling around on the library stairs. Stormy was drinking beer with the boys, they all drank Budweiser, clutching the red white & blue cans. We were trying to see if the baby really had that tattoo but we didn't want them to catch us looking. Stormy was getting drunker and drunker and horsing around with the boys and the baby was crawling around like a wind-up toy, down the stairs, headed for the sidewalk. It was terrifying that this girl was a mother. Anyone could have just scooped that kid up and been gone with it. Justine eventually did, before the baby ended up squashed by someone running for the bus. She lifted the child and brought it back up the stairs and Stormy was immediately there, furious, Budweiser can in hand. We had touched the baby. Now she had to kill us. That's when it got bad, when we forced them to acknowledge us by touching the tattooed baby. They knew we were scared. They were like dogs, a pack of mean dogs. Once they smelt us shrink back we were doomed. They took two of us, Mike and Yvonne. They were like the king and queen of our little gothic world, not because they were benevolent or good leaders but because they both had the biggest black hair and seemed considerably more disturbed than the rest of us, and that commanded respect. They huddled together and cried a lot. The skinheads took Mike and Yvonne and dumped them in the river. Just lifted them, kicking and screaming, and dropped them in. It was so humiliating it was nearly impossible to imagine. Part of Mike and Yvonne's dignity was that they barely ever spoke. It was blasphemy that they had been made to yell and beg and scream. I personally missed most of the big skinhead scares that summer. Since quitting my job at the Square Deal I'd been hired and fired by a gourmet ice cream shop in Fanueil Hall, so I had no money to get into Boston and of course no money to drink. It was hot like it gets in Boston, the air all thick and wet and sitting heavy on your skin. School was out and I hung out at home eating Kraft macaroni and cheese and playing Trivial Pursuit with my sister. So I wasn't there for the big attack, when they got Rachel on the ground and tried to rip her boots from her feet. They were always threatening to steal our boots but that was the first time they actually tried it. We all wore Doc Martins and the skinheads thought Doc Martins were skinhead things and we had no right. They ripped out chunks of Rachel's spidery hair, and another girl also got punched and had her hair ripped out. It was so scary to hear about; these were my friends. Peter was there, he ran to his car, pulled it up to the front of the library and yelled for everyone to jump in. Everyone ran, all these big hairdos darting towards safety and the skinheads right behind them kicking Peter's car, grabbing onto it as if they could stop it from moving. I was petrified. I told my parents about it. I wanted a knife and my father was a big fan of self-defense, he had a couple of knives, I thought they'd want to help me out. They went crazy. What kind of war zone was I hanging out in. I wasn't allowed to go into Boston anymore. I was crying in my living room, my parents were drunk, had been out at this shabby bar called Dick's that had an adjacent pizza parlor, and the scene just spun out of my grasp. It was manic, my parents yelling about how I ask for trouble, looking so weird. It was not the first time I'd gone to my parents for help and ended up worse than I'd started. *A knife!* my mother kept yelling. *A knife!* I had this habit then, of scratching my neck when I was scared or had lost control of my surroundings, and I was sitting in the worn wool armchair just digging at my neck with my fingernails. I wanted them to stop me but they didn't. They were just insane, the both of them but especially my mother, because her mother had just died of cancer and she had enough to deal with without me and knives. Joez was over that night, she was cowering in the doorway like they were going to come after her next. *Come on* said my mother, *we're going for a drive.* She was wrecked. What About Joez I asked and she said *Joez, wait here.* I went out front, I was barefoot, my mother was crying. She kept yelling at me. I just turned and left. Amazing to realize I could do that. Even as my naked feet carried me to the park down the street I couldn't believe I was getting away with it. I sat on a swing and cried. I didn't understand what had happened. A gang of nazis had attacked my friends and I was scared and then my parents lost it. And I had left poor Joez alone with them. I had to go back. I snuck up the back stairway and into my room where Joez sat on the floor, listening to records and writing her name on the linoleum in wet blobs of black nail polish. I sat down beside her and lit a Marlboro Light and cried and said She's Crazy She's Crazy She's Just Crazy and Joez lit a stick of incense, Courage the package read, I had bought it at one of the secret witch shops in Salem. *Yeah,* she said, *I've never seen anyone so crazy.*

The skinheads were gone by the end of the summer. They just up and left to terrorize some other place. I think that once they realized what truly easy targets we were they got bored. After the major boot and hair ripping attack they left us alone, although one boy named Lou came close to getting pummeled. Lou used to be my boyfriend, I was drunk and in love with him for about two weeks, the maximum time I could spend with a boy before the curious panic set in and I'd have to end it. I was breaking up with Lou, we were both drunk of course and he was crying and saying *why why* and I was crying and saying It's Me It's Me. We were making out and sobbing and finally I said That's It We're Broken Up and I left. And Lou went over to where the skinheads were lurking with their patriotic cases of beer and he started screaming at them. He was calling them Roll On Deodorants. Obviously he was suicidal and no one understood why they didn't just kill him. He was this scrawny little boy, scraggly hair and old men's clothes, probably a fag. We tried to fuck once but he couldn't get hard and we went and told everyone we had done it anyway cause we were sick of being virgins. Lou was really sweet. The skinheads could have torn him apart but they didn't. They just drank their beers and laughed at him.

Even after the skinhead army left town there were still

these individual ones who would pop up and terrorize you. There was Luke, who me and Joez would run into as we roamed around Boston. The seething tourist coliseum of Fanueil Hall where people would take our picture. At first it was flattering because it meant we had succeeded in looking like freaks, but eventually the tourists and their cameras annoyed us, and we would yell at them, throw our food at them, cover our faces like big stars. Finally we got smart and started charging money. On weekends we'd make enough for cigarettes and french fries and sweaty wax cups of coke. We would walk over to the swarming hive of Downtown Crossing and eat in the food court of the cavernous mall there, walk further down Washington Street to the edge of the combat zone, where for a little while there was a really great Goodwill. I got lots of dresses there, gauzy black with bows and beads, really old and stinking like grandmothers. Good clunky jewelry. The Boston Common was there to sit down in and smoke, then Newbury Street with its great stretch of magnificent windows and, up at the top, Copley. Luke would be downtown a lot, sitting on benches, smoking. He looked pretty fucked up, ragged in his filthy clothes and bald head. We understood it straight off that he was crazy, crazy in a way that you had to be nice to. Like a vicious dog you have to let smell your hand so he won't attack you. Luke hated everyone he didn't know so you had to make sure you knew him and gave him cigarettes when you passed his sulky bench. He scoffed at our Marlboro Lights in their white and gold boxes. He smoked them, though. Luke was poor. He got kicked out of his house a long time ago, told us about how he ate cold Chef Boy-Ar-Dee raviolis straight from the can on his sixteenth birthday. Alone on the sidewalk like he always was. Luke got a crush on Joez and that was scary. He was a boy you prayed would not get a crush on you because it was like you'd have no choice but to go along with it. *Great, the bald psycho's stalking me* Joez'd say when we'd see him lumbering up to us. It's actually kind of amazing that Joez didn't go out with him. She seemed so defeated, and so desperate for a boyfriend. *What would you do,* Peter asked, *if you were in this big warehouse and there was a serial killer in there with you and he'd cut the power and the electricity, what would you do?* Peter always asked questions like this. *I would lie down,* Joez said, *and just let him kill me.* Joez! I yelled at her. You're Supposed To Think Of A Smart Way Out! She shrugged. Joez thought she was ugly, thought boys wouldn't ever like her. I couldn't believe hearing that, I had just assumed Joez knew she was the pretty half of our friend couple, I'd been happy that she never really mentioned it. How do you make a girl know she's beautiful. What is the system for that, what do you show her, how do you give her a new set of eyes and turn her face back to the mirror. Joez cried so much now. But she knew to stay away from skanky Luke. *Why don't you want to go out with me.* Luke broke his arm skateboarding, or maybe it was his leg or ankle. He was moving around in a cast for a while, some dirty plastic anchor that made him slower and eas-ier to avoid. We didn't know Luke was a skinhead til he told us. I don't think I took it seriously, I thought he'd just seen that news show about them and was trying to be bad. There was a guy named Victor who worked the out-door carts downtown and he was a skinhead too. Again, I didn't learn this til later. Lots of kids in Boston wore flight jackets, suspenders. I had known Victor forever when he pulled his silver medallion out from his shirt and showed me the swastika. *I'm a nazi* he said proudly. He had an incredibly raspy voice like Wolfman Jack. Very short, dark skin like Italian, stocky, big fuzzy eyebrows. Bald head, swastika tucked under his collar. I didn't know what to say. Why, I asked. *I hate Jews.* Why, I asked again. I didn't get it. I was really disappointed. I thought he was smart but I was wrong, he was dumb. I shrugged. That Doesn't Make Any Sense I said with that little knot you get your belly when things like that happen. He laughed. He was really sinister now, and I made sure to avoid him. Luke, who had changed his full title to Luke The Last because he was the last real skinhead, went away to Chicago and Joez got to relax. He came back years later and he was noticeably crazier, more violent, and he got a crush on Julie who had skin like the thinnest white eggshell. Cool-colored veins ran beneath her lids and temples. Her hair was also fragile and white and held back with velvet. She was Ukrainian and her real name was Eustina. I wasn't sure about her. She was really uptight in that girly way, like she would tap me and whisper *the way you're sitting, you can see your underwear,* and I would shift in my skirt and feel weird for not really caring. Once I watched her put on lipstick before she ate. Eustina was dating Peter who was actually gay and madly in love with Madonna in that gay-boy way, and Eustina did in fact look like her. Peter filmed a video of her climbing all over his car, lip-synching to *Burning Up.* So Luke got a fixation on her and I believe he threw a brick through Peter's car window. Something bad happened. He kept asking Justine if she wanted him to beat up Peter for her and she would explain, *No, I like him.* Luke was dying to beat up Peter. We were all very scared for him, but nothing happened, Luke just faded away again and then the next thing I heard about him was incredible. He was hanging out with Patrick who was gay and into fucking lots of boys and talking about it loudly. I loved Patrick. He looked like Pee-Wee Herman and was funny in that gay way. Luke was homeless and sleeping in Patrick's bed. They cuddled. Nu-uh, I said. You're Kidding. He shook his head. But He's A Skinhead, He Hates Gay People. *Oh he's the biggest closet case walking.* Every night Patrick would try to get Luke to suck his dick and Luke wouldn't. Are You Lying To Me I demanded *Swear to god.* Luke wouldn't do it but he kept coming back each night to sleep in Patrick's bed and cuddle like he was a normal human animal with feelings. It was just too weird. I didn't see Luke again til a couple years ago, out front of a cafe on Haight Street. I was drinking coffee with my girlfriend, we were both watching the weird guy circling the sidewalk like a carnivorous bird. No Way, I Know Him! He was still bald, and he looked like he had lost his mind completely. Crazy piercing eyes that cut into you and looked nowhere. He was wearing this long black coat, very dramatic, and had rings of feather and bone piled around his neck. He was holding a big painting of a goat head with all these satanic marks on it, he'd walk up to people drinking their coffee and hold it up at them, walk away muttering. I kept waiting for him to hit someone. I Know Him, I said.

I need to get back to Joez and tell you more things. I have to tell you about the house she lived in, in Salem, with her mom with the poverty agenda, her dad that didn't talk, and her two older sisters — the one who helped run Dukakis's run for president and the reason for all the Dukakis propaganda on the fridge and in the window, and the other one who liked folk music and was boring, seemed kind of lesbian to me though I never said this to Joez. Joez's sisters thought she was a mess, between them and her parents she barely left her room all week, she shut herself in there and listened to records, practiced her bass, and cried a whole lot. Sometimes she'd call me, all hiccupy in the middle of one, and sometimes she'd just mention it later, when she was calm again. Joez's house wasn't like my house, but then Salem wasn't like Chelsea. Chelsea was poor, a bad city getting worse, Getting Out Of Chelsea was something my family talked about a lot, a kind of sport. Keeping tabs on who was winning, what families recently Got Out, you either rooted for them, *Good fa them*, or you hated them, *Ah, money goes ta money.* Joez's family wasn't very rich at all, but Salem was a calm and pretty place to live, and they owned their house and it was beautiful. It was a big wooden castle with a brilliant stained glass window, fan-shaped and every color. Salem, as you know, is a very historical city, and tourist trolleys would cruise by and people would take pictures of Joez's fancy house. Her parents had tried to get it declared a historical monument but the Chamber of Commerce said it wasn't old enough, so they were bitter. Joez would stand in her front yard and stick her middle finger up at all the tourists' cameras. Many years ago the house had been a boarding house, so all the bedrooms had these small white sinks with little mirrors. Joez's was covered with a soft film of the baby powder she dusted her face with to keep it looking dead. She had

Siouxsie posters on her walls and lots of good records. One 4th of July she got her parents to let her throw a BBQ party and invite all her friends from the city. We packed Peter's truck with cases of wine coolers for later when we would go to the beach and take acid and drink. It was weird to be at Joez's house with all the kids from the library steps. Joez's mom was tense and smiling, bringing plates of grilled chicken and bowls of onion dip onto the porch. Peter was running around with his video camera and the *Rocky Horror* people were choreographing dances on the lawn. Everything was perfect and then it went Splat. Percy was scheduled to show up later with acid, he called during the party to ask how many hits he should bring. Of course Joez's mother was listening on the other line. I was in the living room when I heard Joez scream my name, a loud sob. Upstairs, Joez was in her mother's room, shades down, lights off. It was dark and she was crying, covering her round powdered face with her hands. Her mother looked at me. *I just heard my Jennifer make a drug deal* she said dramatically. Kind of accusingly. *Please tell your friends to leave. MOM!* Joez wailed. *You can stay* she said sternly, *but everyone else goes*. Downstairs Joez's father was clapping his hands together saying *party's over*. Peter caught that moment with his video camera, the big white-haired Dad and all the nervous *Rocky Horror* kids solemnly collecting their things from the lawn. I did not want to stay. It was like I was being punished too and they weren't even my parents. I had 10 bucks invested in the booze in Peter's trunk and I knew everyone would get drunk without me. Joez's parents stood on the porch observing the silent departure. You could tell they thought we all were trash. In the living room I facilitated the dysfunctional family therapy session. Joez sobbed, her mother said sharp, mean things about her hair, and her father sat unspeaking. I tried to explain. I was kind of Joez's lawyer. It was so tragic. Joez had never even done acid before. It was going to be her very first trip and of course no one believed her. Now her mom thought she was a junkie. *I knew you were hanging out with druggies* she spat. *We're not druggies, do we look like druggies?* Joez cried. *No Jenny you look like bankers!* She didn't get punished. I think her parents thought she was too far gone for punishment, but she had to live there in that house with them thinking she was such a loser. Joez eventually got to try acid and it was terrible, she was paranoid the whole time. She kept saying *what if I have a bad trip* right up until she peaked. Someone commented that people with chemical imbalances shouldn't do drugs, and people started calling Joez 'Chemicals' and she hated it.

We all kept getting a little older and Joez kept getting a little more depressed. She would cry and tell me how sad she was and then yell at me for never sharing my own sadness with her. But I wasn't sad. I was actually a little embarrassed at my cheerfulness. I felt like a poseur. I should have been wearing pink. Joez sat in her dark dark clothes and drank with Renee Blue Hair who was giving her valium or xanax or something. Joez Don't, I said. *Oh what do you know Michelle* she said and bitterly ate her pill. Renee turned out to be a dyke so I guess that's why she was so upset. I saw her years later at a pro-choice rally and I could tell she'd been anorexic by the way her teeth sat so large in her face. Joez was always badly wanting a boyfriend. Who wasn't. For a little while she was obsessed with Chris, who looked so much like Morrissey I'm sure he was gay. All the boys looked like Morrissey or else like Robert Smith and certainly all of them were gay. Joez said she was going to marry the first guy who asked her. Joez Don't, I said, and she rolled her eyes. Big grey eyes framed by all that makeup. At night in my room she'd have wads of toilet paper, wiping all the paint from her face. She'd leave smudgy tissues all over the floor, I'd walk around barefoot with one stuck to my heel. They were in my bed amongst the blankets. Sometimes, I'd be half dozing off and feel the mattress lift as Joez stumbled out of the room and into the bathroom to puke. Joez's hangover's were heavier than mine. It was hard to get her up in the morning, so I'd lie there for a while, reading. Sometimes my mother would open the door and say *up and at 'em. Rise and shine. You're not going to sleep the day away you two, this isn't a flophouse. This room smells like alcohol breath*, she sniffed. Mom, I groaned. She was petrified of me ending up an alcoholic like everyone else in the family.

When did Joez become too much. She was truly tormented now, and made the biggest deal about drinking. We all did it, but the way she talked about it so much. If we didn't want her to come along we'd lie and say we weren't going to drink and she'd get pissed and say *Fine*, all snippy. She thought it was a sell-out thing to do, like when I started wearing colors. She felt so betrayed, but I couldn't sit there in time with her forever. I was wearing jeans and she was yelling at me for it. Angry at my red shirt. She started hanging out with these mean looking industrial kids who had an industrial computer band. She was with them at a party, they all glared at me. Joez, I said, catching her in the hallway. I Don't Want To Be Your Enemy. *You're not* she said simply, and that was it. They used to crank call me at 3 in the morning, threatening to kick my head in, telling me to brush my teeth. I was hurt and scared but really I couldn't be too upset because I crank called people too. Eventually they stopped.

After I graduated high school I spent some time fucking around at a cafe, fixing sandwiches, brewing coffee, getting a boyfriend. His name was Ian, he came in around the holidays with a christmas card for me, an evil-looking angel balancing a tree ornament on his finger. The angel had liquidy black eyes and an Elvis Presley pompadour, and Ian had made the card himself. He was an art student. He lived in a big house over in Dorchester, Savin Hill, an area he called Stab-n-Kill. That day that Ian came into my cafe he had a friend with him, and he said to his friend as they pushed open the glass door, *I'm gonna get her, 'cause I'm a pioneer.* Something like that. He gave me the card and told me he was on his way out to Route 1 in Saugus, to go to the giant Salvation Army there, and I was impressed that he knew about Route 1. It's this neon strip of theme restaurants — The Ship, which is an actual ship; The Leaning Tower of Pizza with the crooked monument growing from its roof; Weylus' — a paradisical pagoda with a stream running through the inside, and ornate golden statues of swirling dogs and flaming dragons. *Do you want anything from the Salvation Army?* he asked, and I said Rosary Beads, and he came in the next day with a holy necklace that looked like a string of black tic-tacs, interrupted here and there with pious metal medallions. For our first date we went to the Chil-

44

dren's Museum with the giant milk bottle out front, and inside Ian stole me a piece of lamb vertebrae from the skeleton exhibit. When the place closed up we went back to his place in Dorchester, we sat on his futon which was folded up like a couch, and we drank beer and I let him rummage around under my shirt. Ian was my boyfriend. After about two weeks I decided that I was in love with him, so that we could have sex. There was a 70s party at his house, I was in a scratchy gold dress with worn-down gold pumps, and I grabbed Ian in the dark kitchen and said I Love You. It meant You Can Fuck Me Now. We did it in his room, to the epic drama of Kiss Me Kiss Me Kiss Me, the crashing red and orange sounds and Robert's mournful voice and I didn't come and I hadn't really expected to, but Ian had just assumed I had had an orgasm, and when I said No, I Didn't the next day at the kitchen sink, doing dishes, he was upset. I Still Had Fun, I said, half-defensive, half-comforting. I Still Want To Do It Again. *I can't believe you didn't come.* Was he angry? Girls Don't Come From Just Being Fucked, I said. I had read this in Cosmo. I remember Joez telling me that there were no nerve endings up there, if there were you'd just about die for real having a baby. I told all of this to Ian. *All my other girl-friends came that way.* Bitches, I thought. I joined their ranks. The next time me and Ian did it, this time to the Last Temptation of Christ soundtrack, I pretended to. *See,* he smiled. So I quit that cafe and I got a Good Job, a job with benefits, a job that vaguely utilized the graphic arts training I had gotten in high school. It was at a publishing house that published trade magazines for industries I didn't really understand. Some were

45

about computers, which I could grasp, but the others were foreign, engineering or something, and all the magazine titles were abbreviations that did nothing to clue you into their content. There was a copy editor who sometimes came down to my department, she was young and snotty with long blonde hair. I remember her telling me she was quitting because she couldn't align her politics with the pro-weaponry, anti-environment articles. Really I still have no idea what kind of horror I was temporarily a part of. I do remember waxing up a piece about how to dispose of toxic waste inexpensively.

My position within the publishing house was basically unnecessary, I was a luxury for the paste up artists. I ran sheets of text through a waxing machine, trimmed it up and left it on a shelf. Mostly I sat in my cubicle writing stories about straight girls with terrible boyfriends, and read everyone's tarot cards. I was sort of a mascot — the paste up artists, all women, got a hoot out of me. Babette, whose boyfriend had broken up with her a million years ago but still the pain of it weighted her head to her desk. I'd walk into her cubicle to bum a piece of candy off her and she'd be hunched over, a kind of corporate pieta, that frozen sorrow. Elsie had more life in her, she'd tell me the stories her mother had told her, all the crazy things she'd seen growing up in Haiti. Women who'd been hexed giving birth to babies with tails, stories about zombies and how Elsie and her sister had special pouches hung around their necks for protection. *Gris-Gris* she said, a word impossible for me to pronounce. Debbie was really a mess, she was like the department whore. We'd cram into her cubicle to be horrified and entertained by her tales of last night's casual sex, guys she met in bars of course but also in grocery stores or public transportation, everywhere. These women thought I was kind of weird but in an excusable, young way. They'd come into my cubicle to gawk at the walls, which had been arranged into a type of pop culture museum with pictures of Madonna and the many actors of *Twin Peaks*, anonymous models decked out in John Paul Gaultier, drag queens torn from the pages of Details before it went boy. I was their MTV. Once one of the big bosses, so big no one really knew who he was, had seen me walking across the parking lot in a hot pink girdle I sometimes wore as a skirt, and word was sent down the corporate hierarchy that if I ever wore it again I would be sent home without pay. It was a big exciting scandal that everyone in the company had their own opinion on. The paste up ladies were very supportive but outside that little circle I was openly disliked, because I was young and frivolous and didn't care about the company and was getting paid pretty well to do nothing. These workers surely saw me as someone passing through while they were there for the long haul, with their computers and their coffee mugs.

I made two genuine friends at the publishing house, and both were named Tina. One Tina was a typesetter, she was a radical activist and listened to NPR as she typed. This was during the Gulf War when whole departments were arranging cardboard boxes for the soldiers, canned food and magazines and pantyhose to be stretched over guns to filter out sand. Tina had petitions about Bush and about the war and later, when the troops were sent home and everyone was wearing yellow ribbons, Tina had petitions to drop charges on her radical friends who had soaked the New York victory parade in blood-red paint balloons.

My other friend named Tina worked in the art department, the only member of that team who was truly an artist. She brought in slides of her work and it was brilliant. Cubist I think, but maybe that's just because there were lots of squares in them. All these murky colors, greens and blues, big blocks containing men with huge dicks, women who appeared to be trapped. Women trapped by huge cubist dicks. Tina was obviously tormented. She was intensely sexual, probably a scorpio. She talked about sex a lot. She had this boyfriend Chris and I heard quite a bit about him, how they played out these doctor fantasies and he'd slap her cunt with a wooden tongue depressor. She said it felt good, urged me to try it. Tina was the only woman I knew who had done it with another woman, and this was the root of the fixation which I developed on her. I wouldn't call it a crush, though at first it may have been. The feelings were intense, this ocean I was on the verge of plunging into. I had messed around with a girl once before, Nadia. She was Ian's old girlfriend. He was certain she'd fuck a girl because once at boarding school she had watched her roommate masturbate. She'd told him this. Nadia was this really sweet, kind of hippiesh girl whose mother had died a long time ago and she lived with her father and never had any female role models and that was why she liked to fool around with girls. She told this to me and Ian as we passed a fat green 40 of Heffenreffer around the alley behind the movie theater in Harvard Square. Ian kissed Nadia. Right in front of me, there on the dirty steps by the big smelly dumpsters that contained leftover popcorn and many rats. It was interesting to see what Ian looked like when he made out. I always had my eyes closed, plus you just can't tell from that particular angle. He looked kind of ravenous. *Now you two* he said, pulling away. He still looked ravenous. Nadia kissed me. It was pretty great. She tasted like skanky beer and clove cigarettes and girl, we kissed a long time and then took turns kissing Ian, and then the three of us went to North Station to wait with Nadia for her train back to Ipswich. On the rocky train tracks she laid down like a tied-up damsel, and Ian and I tugged her jeans down to her thighs and with wet hands fought for the space between her legs. Then the train came, and Nadia was gone. This event seemed destined to never happen again, but here was Tina. We'd eat lunch together and I'd earnestly try to steer the conversation towards bisexuality. I'm Bisexual, I confessed. It was my big pickup line. I told her about Nadia, my single contribution to our sex dialogue. Tina was considerably older than me and had a real head start, sexually speaking. I'd just sit and listen, leaf with fascination through the sex catalogues she let me borrow, ordered from the back of Cosmopolitan. They advertised dildoes, butt-plugs, restraints, and were the closest thing to pornography I'd ever kept in my room. I looked through them before sleeping, they turned me on terribly. I couldn't figure out what the leather slings were for but I knew it was awful. I'm Bisexual I said to Tina, a gigantic thing for me to say at the time. It meant I Want To Fuck You. I had a feeling Tina wanted to fuck me too but she was a package with her boyfriend the way I was a package with Ian. They'd sleep with other couples sometimes, Tina had

told me about how they did it with her new roommate
JP who was so anal she yelled at someone for not tossing out the bottlecap immediately after cracking open a
beer. JP worked at the publishing company too and
acted really snobby to me. I knew it was because I was
so young and Tina liked me and she was jealous. JP was
plain looking and obviously boring, she dressed in tans
and browns and I knew that if Tina slept with her she'd
definitely sleep with me. But a scene with her boyfriend
was out of the question. That was not how things
worked with Ian. We were non-monogamous, a new
idea. I was taking books out of the library about it, really
trying to figure it out and do it right. But we were a very
special kind of non-monogamous — girls were fine, but
boys were out of the question, unless Ian needed to further explore his sexuality by sleeping with one. The obvious unfairness of this was irritating, and when I tried to
talk to Ian about it he turned jealous, and angry, and the
conversation became two or three hours of me assuring
Ian he was the only boy I wanted to sleep with. Which
was true. I wasn't liking boys so much, especially after
finding girls, so why bother. And we were able to snare
Tina without her boyfriend. She was house-sitting an
apartment in a very quaint part of Boston, Bay Village.
We were sitting out on a back porch walled with plants
and flowering vines. It was spring and I was telling her
about this dream I had where I was kissing Oprah Win-
frey. Another desperate attempt to steer conversation
towards my desire for her. I just could not say it. Let me
tell you what Tina looked like. She was thin. She looked
like a hungry deer, those big brown eyes. Short hair colored red, professionally, in a salon. She dressed funny,

50

even by my standards. She'd talk forever about all the great clothes she got on the trip to Europe that ruined her credit history, all these amazing outfits she charged that were then stolen from her car at the airport in New York City. Tina drove this crappy little car, she drove me and Ian to the combat zone to go to a porn store. That's how it happened. Ian was a great porn aficionado and Tina wanted some for her art, among other reasons. And I like to go places I've never been. It was a good outing. We walked through Chinatown on the way to the shop and Tina was pointing into alleys telling us how bombs had blown up here and there because these different organized crime gangs were at war and it was in the papers and you didn't know when they would strike next, and that just made the whole trip so much more exciting, walking through the dirty, narrow streets and thinking we could all be accidentally killed.

At the porn store I was vaguely embarrassed and unsure of how to conduct myself. I mean, do you just stand around and browse, flip through the magazines like you would at a newsstand? I honestly didn't have much interest in anything they were selling. The dildoes looked so cold. None of the women in the girl-girl books looked like women I'd want to fuck. Even the punk ones looked contrived. There were some bondage magazines, arty photos of women binding each other with intricately knotted rope. Those were intriguing, but I was more interested in what went on once the women were safely tied. The rope seemed to be an end to itself. The back room was the SM room. All the gear was leather and very expensive, a little bald man had to let us in with a key. Tina knew what everything was for. She even owned nipple clamps and a ball gag. She told me they sold Snake Bite Kits because you could put the yellow suction cup on your nipple and it felt good. She owned one of those, too. Back at her house I discovered it in a basket by her futon. It was so goofy-looking, this bright yellow plastic. I was fooling around with it, sticking it on my forehead, and it left a dumb red circle like a hickey. We fucked, all three us, on her futon with a blue light glowing. How could it not be disappointing, the anticipation was so great. Ian's involvement made the whole thing seem choreographed, we had to keep coming up with positions that included him. He fucked Tina doggy-style while she attempted to lick my clit, her face banging into me with each of his thrusts. Later she said she felt like an electrical conductor connecting me and the boy, sending our energy back and forth through her body. That wasn't what it was like for me at all.

I really pursued the thing with Tina, I chased her, kept it going. I felt like there was something there for me in women and Tina was a woman so why was it that the idea was better than the reality. It was like if I want women I should want all women. Something like that. I was reading Anaïs Nin's diaries at the time, that's what I was trying to make it. Romantic, french. The morning after we slept together I found a flower on my light table at work. That helped. And that she was an artist helped as well. I'd always wanted to be made immortal, a muse. She wanted to paint us, me and Ian. We sat for her one night in the chill of her basement, I was wearing this blue and black striped dress I found in the reduced bin at Betsey Johnson. It's what she wanted to paint me in. The portrait was never completed because we couldn't sit still, so antsy to see if we would all sleep together again, that night. We didn't. Tina felt guilty, she was cheating on her boyfriend. Her therapist thought she might be a sex addict, she sexualized all her relationships. We did go to see Billy Idol together, the three of us. She drove us north to the outdoor stadium in her sputtering little car. The show sucked, it was cold and I was in this tiny plastic miniskirt. It rained and Billy Idol was such a dork, he kept referring to his dick and pretending to fuck the enormous blow up doll stage set. How disappointing to see your adolescent hero for the asshole he truly is. It was his Cyberpunk tour, it affirmed for the public that Billy's career was really over. On the drive home we were trying to get Tina to pull over and have sex in the car. She held out; her boyfriend, her therapist. She came into my house to use the bathroom and it was great to introduce my parents to a woman I was kind of having an affair with.

The publishing company was having financial troubles and laying everyone off. There were woman crying in the stalls in the bathroom. I was certain I'd get canned, seeing how I didn't really do anything, but in the big picture my salary was so small they might as well keep me. Tina was a freelancer so they brought her in less frequently. But even when she wasn't on an assignment she would come by and take me to lunch. By then I was not only over Tina, I was confused as to what it had been about in the first place. She was a symbol. Had our sex been safe? Tina fucked a lot of people. It made me panicky to think about. I began avoiding our lunch dates. Eventually she moved away, to graduate school in San Antonio. She sent me a letter once, a card she made herself, a drawing of me and Billy Idol. It looked really cool. She sent it with a stone cross on a rope to wear around my neck. I wore it for a while and then I lost it.

* ★ *

Because I had a Real Job with a Real Salary, and still lived at home with my parents, rentless, and Ian had only a crappy customer service job at Copy Cop, with not only rent, bills and car-related expenses to consider but also all the additional expenses of being an Artist — brushes, paints, canvases — I was the one who funded our vacation to Montreal. Oh, Montreal was great. There was this comedy festival happening, the temperature was over 100 degrees and the place was packed with tourists. The city was experiencing a massive, record breaking heat wave and there was no place to swim. We went to the botanical garden and dunked our heads in the fountain with all the ducks; we popped into cool glass ATM rooms to wipe ourselves off and breathe. We took the subway to the underground shopping malls that were cathedral-like and air conditioned, and that's where I was when I started crying again. It was because of The Pill. I had been on it once before, months ago, when I first met Ian. It had me locking myself in restaurant bathrooms, unable to get out of bed or off the curb and onto the bus because I just could not stop crying. My face was bloated and red as a newborn at all times because I was either just calming down from or rushing into another one of these fits. Everyone was worried about me. In high school I had had this friend named Tracey, she was always at my house and freaking out, no one really knew why. She'd storm down my front stairs at 8am, swearing and crying, waking everyone up. I was on my bed in the midst of one of my fits, sobbing, ripping out my hair, and my mother stood in the doorway, teeth clenched, saying *Don't pull a Tracey, Michelle.* On the other side of the doorway was a kitchen filled with people eating pizza in celebration of one of my sister's events, a dance recital or beauty pageant or something. And I couldn't eat my pizza, I was losing my mind and my mother was in the doorway, half worried, half angry because I was taking the normality out of her life. It was not normal to have a daughter so tormented. She got me off the bed and drove me to a hospital in Boston, to get blood work done. Maybe I had a hormonal imbalance, the technicians weren't sure. My mother was sure. She had had a hysterectomy, and if she didn't wear her estrogen patch she went crazy. Whenever I was upset it was my hormones — my mother, child of the 50s, parroting back at me this classic dismissal of female discontent. Eventually she took me back to the doctor who had given me The Pill in the first place. Dr. Brown, I hated her. She had given me my first gyn exam, poking around inside me saying things like *This shouldn't hurt, it's no bigger than your boyfriend's penis* and *You know, you don't have to shave yourself there.* I Know That, I snapped. Ian thought it was cool, a shaved pussy. So my mother brought me back to her, I was sitting on the exam table with my clothes on, hostile and stuffy from crying. *Your mother tells me you're feeling kind of blue,* she said. Kind of blue. I wanted to die, I was so miserable. She took me off the pill and gave me a prescription for Prozac that I promptly tossed out the car window on the drive home. What Kind Of Doctor Are You Taking Me To, I demanded. Prozac. I watched Oprah. People on Prozac went homicidal. I didn't need to make things more difficult. At least I was only hurting myself.

55

I stopped eating The Pills. My periods came back longer and heavier, and the crying stopped. I felt pretty ok. I started thinking maybe it hadn't been the pills after all, maybe it had been other stuff that I'd worked out in my head. I got another prescription from another doctor, and I was popping them through Montreal where I was vacationing with Ian. I was sitting in the food court, drinking a coke and I just burst out crying all over my taco. Ian started freaking out, saying *Just stop taking them stop taking them right now*. I just stared at him, the salty water dribbling down my face. Ian wanted to have sex all the time. If we were left alone for more than five minutes his hand would be on the black denim crotch of his jeans and zip whing his cock was out and I would be expected to do something with it. I was his girlfriend. After some time of this I had learned about the different ways to take care of Ian and his dick, and I had settled on fucking. Blow jobs numbed my mouth and gagged me, my hands would smell like stale saliva afterwards, and I really hated the musty stink of Ian's groin. How is it that girls have gotten the big stinky genitalia rap, while everybody pretends that boys don't smell exactly like moldy mushrooms from the back of the crisper drawer down there. Hand jobs sucked because my arm got cramped and it was so weird to watch Ian laid back on pillows, sighing and happy like a baby getting his diaper changed. Anal sex was out of the question, and this was a big tragedy for Ian since it was actually his favorite sexual activity. Ian kept coming up with these new ways to try it that would make it not hurt so much — getting me drunk, applying Ambusal, that gum-numbing stuff, to my resistant butthole, but none of it worked. Regular fucking required minimal effort on my part, I could simply lie there, and sometimes it felt good. No Pills equaled less fucking and more of the other stuff. Ian was stormy. *I don't know why you started taking them again when you know what they do to you.* I hated him. He just wanted an easy life and a girl that was happy all the time. He didn't understand what I was going through at all. It was like having intense PMS forever. How you want everyone to be as miserable as you are. When these fits kicked in I would just put Ian through hell. He really did deserve it, I knew this, though it would have been difficult for me to explain why. It was intuitive. We sat in our hotel room with the AC on, playing poker and getting drunk on some fruity liquor that this strange city decided I was old enough to buy. Finally having sex, which included me putting the empty liquor bottle into my cunt because he wanted me to and I thought I was supposed to like it. There was a lot that I was supposed to like that I didn't.

At night we went to gay bars. I looked up BARS in the yellow pages and called until I found a gay one. It was bingo night, a drag queen in a blond wig and lashes calling out the numbers in french, and me and the boy trying to figure out what she was saying. The bar loved us. We were this cute American couple, a boy and a girl, playing bingo in a gay bar. People were translating the bingo numbers for us. The drag queen asked into the microphone *Are you two boyfriend/girl-friend?* I'm Gay I blurted and everyone laughed. It felt like a confession and lie at once. That's what it was. *Well, I myself like MEN*, the queen snorted. Ian made a big show of kissing her cheek as we left and it was like, wow, what a really cool straight boy.

I found a lesbian bar. It was called Kiev and the walk from the hotel brought us by these beautiful french canadian homes with lacy wrought iron stairs that reached down to the street. Even at night it was so hot, my hair in a ponytail that stuck to the sweat on the back of my neck. I took the boy to the lesbian bar. I called first to ask if it was ok and the bartender said yes. Her name was Louise, she said *Come introduce yourselves when you get here.* Louise was nice. She looked like Tina from the publishing company. They had the same big eyes planted on a thin, tanned face. Louise liked me. I could tell. She kept giving us free kamakazees. Kamakazees were all the rage in Montreal, they tasted like lemony cleansers. I was knocking them back, little glasses of them. I couldn't believe this bar, Kiev. It was incredible. All these great-looking women, I couldn't believe they were lesbians. The lesbians I'd glimpsed in Boston seemed to be kind of dull-looking, very academic. These girls at Kiev had style. The cocktail waitresses were the best, they carried around these circular drinktrays covered with graffiti, and would jump into the dance floor and start boogying. They were playing this dance song all the clubs were playing then, it went *I'm a bitch, I-I-I-I-I'm a bitch,* and these waitresses were out there shaking their asses and moving up on each other. I couldn't stop watching. Somewhere in the night Louise kissed me, just a little one, and I kissed her back. Ian was leaving. He was going to a heterosexual punk bar to do the slampit mating dance and impress the ladies with his controlled aggression. He said goodbye to Louise. *There's a fag bar down the street* she suggested. She was being helpful. *Oh, I'm straight* he said, all proud. I wanted to kill him. I was pretending to be a lesbian and he ruined it. A real lesbian would never go vacationing with a straight boy. The jig was up. Louise didn't kiss me again, but she kept handing out the kamakazees. Then this woman who looked like James Dean started passing me cigarettes and buying me shots of tequila. The boy was gone. This woman was so terrific-looking. Short blond hair, leather jacket, white t-shirt. A leather jacket in that incredible heat. Such a dyke. Butch, but I didn't know about that then. She didn't speak english and I didn't speak french so I just kept smoking her cigarettes and smiling at her. When the tequila gave me shudders I clung to her shoulders and laughed, tears shooting from the corners of my eyes. I think she wanted to take me home but I was really too drunk to handle it. I took a cab back to the hotel and the cab driver was a big Celtics fan and all excited that I was from Boston. I Know Nothing About The Celtics I burped from the backseat. I was wrecked. *Oh, Larry Bird, he's a great athlete.* Things Are Cheap Here, I said, But The Sales Tax Is Outrageous. Making my american complaint to this canadian representative. He nodded. *The only ones who can afford to buy anything are the tourists.* I Think I'll Live Here Someday, I said.

The hotel me and Ian were staying at was pretty much in the center of Montreal's red light district. I couldn't get over the hookers. They were all over the place wearing clothes I wished I owned. The street prostitutes in Boston were ragged and strung out on junk but these women were positively fashionable. Clusters of them, up and down that big street in Montreal, Saint

Catherine. The street had a law against standing still, a cop came up and told me to walk. I guess I looked like I could've been one. A woman in front of us was leading a man into a hotel. She wore a long curly wig and this great shiny dress and was patting the guy on the shoulder in this gentle, reassuring way. Look, I said to Ian. I was fascinated. Ian was fascinated with the strip places. They lined the street, alternating with the trendy shops and nightclubs. We went to one. We were the only ones there. It only cost a dollar to get in. We sat at a table and a woman came up to get us a drink. She looked like my old friend Katie, that same bitchy attitude. We didn't want a drink, we were drunk already. She whacked at the card on the table. It said one drink minimum. We'll Split A Beer. *That's one drink each,* she spat. There was a group of mostly naked women crowded around this guy in the corner. One got up and went onto the stage and started dancing. It was this Rod Stewart song that that was a big hit that summer, kind of mellow with a rhythm you could sway to. She was on her hands and knees with her ass to the empty audience, swinging it back and forth then moving like she was being fucked. I do not want to perpetuate the idea of Sex Worker as desperate and miserable, but this woman did not look like she was enjoying herself. I felt sick. I felt so fucked up, I couldn't look at the boy and I couldn't look at the woman and I knew if I opened my mouth the crying would come. I drank my beer. Guns-n-Roses came on and the woman looked a little more lively but it was still depressing. I thought about the woman leading the man into the hotel, and this woman here, unfolding her labia for me and my boyfriend and I thought if I had to

60

choose I'd be a whore. I told this to Ian as we walked back to the hotel and he flipped. He couldn't believe what I was saying, that I was maybe capable of letting anonymous men fuck me. He thought it meant I wanted to. He launched into a descriptive tangent of exactly what it would entail, getting angrier and more disgusting as we walked. I couldn't speak. I was thinking about the millions of times he fucked me and how I always felt nothing and wanted it to be over and probably that's how it was for those women on the street. At the hotel in bed with the air conditioner blasting I laid with my back to him, sobbing into my pillow. I knew he was awake and he knew I was crying and I hated him for not touching me and I would've hated him if he had. I blew snot into the sheets and cried and thought He's Right, I've Got To Stop Taking Those Pills.

* ★ *

Anya was the only lesbian I knew, so she became my girlfriend. There was Tabitha, the quiet goth girl I had begun to awkwardly date after Ian and I returned from Montreal. It had been a vague affair, she had been busy both with her own boyfriend and with art school, but I had heard that she'd found a new girl to go with. Her name was Gretchen — shaved head, tattooed skull. *She hates men*, said Ian, who knew her from art school. Tabitha and Gretchen snorted heroin together, I heard Tabitha's eyes went yellow from it and she really loved the euphoria. Everyone was having an interesting life but me. I was sequestered away at school, Salem State College. I had quit the publishing company and sunk the entirety of my savings into my Education. It seemed to be the thing to do. I always knew I was smart, I was supposed to be the first of my clan to go to college, get a degree, Get Out Of Chelsea. When I was younger I knew a girl, a friend of Joez's, who did a radio show at Salem State, and she was cool so I had it in my head that the school was cool and it was not. It was terribly un-cool. In my History Of Western Civilization class we waited for the teacher to die, he was so old. His deep pauses between breaths had us on the edge of our seats. English was ok, the teacher liked me but thought the way I compared everything to nazi Germany was cliché. Women's Studies was good but frustrating because I just wanted to have sex and it wasn't going anywhere. All the girls had boyfriends. I still had a boyfriend. I had a boyfriend like having a cold that lasts the whole winter. I had a single friend, Caroline, who was also too urban for Salem State. We sat together in her room, but my desperation to get laid prevented any female friendships from really developing. They could smell it. I answered a personal ad. It seemed like such a filthy thing to do, even though it was a very wholesome ad. She was looking for someone creative. I was creative, I was a writer. And nice. I was nice. Laid-back, sure. Friends, maybe more. See how things go, good attitude. I had nothing in common with this woman who worked at a bank, was normal, had one of those Hermès knock-off scarves draped decoratively across the back of her long New England wool coat. It was winter, we went to a restaurant in the North End, The European, ate pasta beneath an enormous fake swordfish. Went back to her apartment and watched Kiss Of The Spider Woman, on video. A gay movie. Made out and felt nothing, no sparks save the residual guilt-thrill of kissing a girl. Maybe I was frigid. Back at my dorm I had all these gay books sitting on my windowsill. Girls with big hair would stop by my room for a tarot reading and see them. *You're inta all kindsa weird shit, huh?* They were reference books. I was doing a report on homophobia for my women's studies class. I was a scholar. After I delivered my presentation my professor came out as a lesbian and I sat there with my heart pounding as all the liberal straight girls demonstrated how openminded they were. *I was watching Tequila Sunrise,* one gushed, *and I couldn't stop staring at Michelle Pfeiffer's legs!*

I would see Anya at all the gay discos. Venus de Milo, Avalon, Axis. I went on the weekends, with Peter who had miraculously also turned out queer and, after a couple of brief and disastrous affairs, was On The Prowl. Sometimes Ian would tag along, and boys would hit on him and he would smile, genuinely flattered, and say *I'm straight.* Ian was cute. I don't think I've mentioned that. He was bald, or had very short hair, bleached, or longer, black, or he had a long red mohawk that could be worn back in a ponytail, or down, hanging greasy over the shaved parts. He had little glasses, wire-rimmed, that made him look smarter than he was, and he had a pair of suspenders, leather, that made him look like a leather fag. His kind of bad skin just made him look rugged. Sometimes Ian came to the clubs with me and Peter, and sometimes he stayed home and made art. I liked those nights best. Like the night I met Anya. You couldn't miss her. She was loud, big wigs, outrageous clothes. She hung out with all these fashion designers, fags that stitched crazy outfits for her to wear out to the clubs. When I met her I asked about lesbian bars and she waved her hand dismissively. *There's Indigo* she said. *All the lesbians hate me there. I'm a fag.* She was a fag, a drag queen. I don't know how we got together, she had it in for me and I just rolled with it. We were in the bathroom at Venus de Milo, location of all my formative homosexual experiences. She was pulling off white satin opera gloves to shove her hand up my cunt. I moved my legs apart and waited for something special to happen. It hurt. Easy, I said, and she scoffed. *That shouldn't hurt* she said authoritatively. *Maybe there's something wrong with you up there.* She picked her gloves off the wet floor and tossed them back down with disgust. I sat on the sink as she washed me off her hands. Then the strut, shaking her tits into my face. I didn't know what femme was then, I just knew it made me uncomfortable when she shimmied up to me like that. It made me feel like a man and I didn't like it. You're So Sexy I said, like I thought I was supposed to. Somewhere there was a script, chartered territory, safety. When the club closed all the fags piled into Peter's car for a drive around the city, making the rounds Peter called it. Me and Anya got the trunk. In the cramped dark it was better. In a space too tight for fucking we made out furiously, our heads hitting the roof as the car dipped into potholes. We went to the Fenway Victory Gardens where boys were fucking in the bushes. We could see their silhouettes against the tall dry weeds, occasionally passed a guy standing alone on the dark path, hands in pockets. My friends thought these boys were so dirty, walking out of the trees with mud on their knees. Ronnie's big hands covered his mouth, caught his shrieking laughter. Me and Anya walked slow with arms tight around each other's waists, kissing and bumping into the boys. Her John Fluevog heels sunk into the dirt, she stumbled. *We're the only girls here* she whispered, giggling. It was a nighttime place, another country, and we were spies.

Anya was a nanny, she lived with this family and had a room of her own hung with pictures of supermodels: Cindy, Naomi, Tatiana, Christy. Madonna was also present. Anya had her own bathroom too, small porcelain sink dusty with different colored powders. She kicked me out. *You can't see me til I'm ready* she said like I was her husband. Anya attached a roll of fake hair to the top of her head, smudged black along her nose to make it look thinner. She was a big german girl from Nebraska whose mother ignored her. *She was never there for me,* Anya called out from behind the bathroom door. *I learned about life from Cosmo and Mademoiselle. Clubs are like magazines come to life.* She came out and touched my hair. *We could give you a beehive* she said. *Well at least wear something different.* None of her clothes fit me. I put on a metallic dress with thin straps that slipped off my shoulders. At the club boys loved us. Sprawled on a couch in the lounge kissing, we come up for air to an audience of eurotrash. *You two are beautiful!* said one boy dramatically. *You are gorgeous!* Anya beamed. At the bar she drank beer and burped loudly. Miss Piggy I teased. Her face darkened. *Don't you ever, ever call me that again* she said in a new, angry voice. *I mean it. OK?* I nodded. *Good.* She smiled and smooched my cheek. Anya looked a lot like Miss Piggy. She really did.

Anya was upset, she might get fired from her nanny job. The family was mad at her, she had left lipstick in her pocket again and it melted over everything in the dryer. She was testy. Allan, her best friend, was having a fashion show that night in this big, cavernous club that only straight people went to. Anya was to model. But at the club something was wrong. It was empty. Bitchy fashion fags were fuming, hurling velvet dresses to the floor in fury. Everyone was making phone calls. They decided to move it to another club, also straight, and have an impromptu performance there. Anya was trying to talk Allan into letting me model too. Allan looked me up and down. *Anya, this is my career* he said tensely. I ended up in some lousy red outfit he wasn't even going to show. A queerly cut vest, new wave, hung on my shoulders like a weird abstract painting. At the club the straight people were annoyed and confused. They wanted to dance but they were herded off the floor by a drag queen in body paint. The DJ popped in Allan's house music tape and all the models got in line to march across the floor. Some girls in platforms eyed me critically and I scowled. I could've looked like that if I'd had more notice. I was wearing sneakers. There was no narration so the whole thing looked bizarre, all these fancy people twirling through a nightclub that by day was actually a restaurant, chairs and tables stacked against the wall. Me in my weird outfit. I made my run across the floor quickly. *You went too fast* Allan complained, and glared at Anya. After the show we stayed at the club and drank for free. The DJ put on rock-n-roll, almost classic rock, as an apology to the straight people. Me and Anya were dancing in between kisses and the boy-girl couples made a big show of their disapproval. Anya lifted my leg and played it like a guitar. She wasn't afraid of making a scene and that I admired. Up at the bar Allan said *Go like this* and put his hands to the side of his face, wiggling his fingers. *Puff your cheeks. Fish,* he laughed. In the car home he said to Anya *Are you going to get your dick out tonight? Has Michelle seen your dick?* Anya laughed and squeezed me. *I've got a big dick* she promised. *It's in a box under my bed.* But in her room we just kissed until we fell asleep. *That's why girls are so great* she murmured drowsily. *We can just do this forever. We don't even need to do anything else.* Anya had these two friends who lived in an expensive apartment in Back Bay. Alexander was tall and swedish-looking, Julian was dark and full-lipped, french and brazilian. They were lovers. Alexander called Anya one afternoon at the nanny house where we were plopped on the couch watching her favorite soap opera. He was hysterical. *Alexander needs me* she said, hanging up. *You can come, he'll buy us dinner.* I don't know if Alexander and Julian were rich or if they were just pretending to be. They lived off credit cards, Alexander's. We met him at a faux french restaurant, he was red-faced and crying in a starched white shirt. *Julian gave me herpes* he sobbed. *Hi Michelle, nice to finally meet you.* Alexander bought us soup and croissants, hot coffee. *The bastard gave me herpes and I just charged him a plane ticket to france!* Alexander was trying to kick Julian out but Julian wouldn't leave. *He has nowhere to go* Alexander wailed. *He was having sex with old men in the mall bathroom!* Alexander was disgusted. The lives of these boys were so odd and intriguing. Julian was gorgeous as a god, he modeled. He didn't need to have sex with old men in mall bathrooms. I nibbled my spinach and cheese croissant and watched Alexander cry. *Will you please come over* he asked. At the apartment Julian was sulking, slamming things around and playing Depeche Mode loud. *How could you do this* Alexander implored, still crying. *How could you?* Alex! Julian said tensely. Please. He was over it. I've got an assignment due tomorrow he said. Julian studied photography at Boston University. He teased and sprayed my hair and painted my face to look like Anya's. Up on the roof he took pictures of us making dangerous faces and kissing. *You look like a doll* said Anya, delighted. I looked at my watch. I Have To Go. I was meeting Ian at North Station, he'd been up on the north shore, visiting his parents. *Can't you cancel* Anya said, annoyed. To Alexander: *She's going to meet her boyfriend.* She was so bothered, but I had told her that very first night, hollering it over the pounding industrial noise mess at Axis, I Have A Boyfriend. And later, to Ian, I Have A New Girlfriend. We were at his house with Nine Inch Nails on his radio and another half-finished portrait of me on his drawing table. In it I was looking up at the fairies that were buzzing around my head, while evil looking snakes slithered down by my neck. It represented my dreamy positivity in the face of all my underlying torment. Ian wanted to hear all about Anya, all the details. I could have been off doing anything, writing in the park, shopping for records, he was that unthreatened by the sex I had with this girl in a bathroom. He actually wanted to meet her, maybe we could all hang out. Maybe, I said. Right. Anya would sooner snip off his mohawk and braid it into hair extensions to wear to her clubs. Back at Alexander's I combed the chemical snarls from my hair. Anya wouldn't look at me. She looked in the mirror. Anya, I Told You I Couldn't Stay All Day. Alexander rubbed her back sympathetically and they took turns glaring at me and Julian. *Bye sweetie* Julian called from the kitchen. I'll Call You I said to Anya and left the apartment.

I never called Anya again. It was real drama — she was princess of every disco in Boston, I would see her there every time, strutting around in her outfits, conferring with her boyfriends. Pretending not to see me. I'd be drinking at the bar and Peter would pinch me — *There's Miss Anya*, and my head would turn and then her head would turn as she buried her mouth in her friend's ear. She actually hit on me again, years later when I looked so different, a big embarrassment for both of us. But Anya wasn't the only girl out at the clubs. I met Kelly in the glinty gold and velvet glamour of Venus De Milo, very dressed up in my shiny white lace dress and the John Fluevog shoes with chesspiece heels that required great skill to walk in. We had danced, Kelly and I, to that awful music all the gay clubs in Boston played, boys blowing whistles and waving their hands above their heads. There was this dance called the runway that the fags destined for New York would do, a snotty strut across the dance floor, a couple runway-model twirls, and another snotty strut back. Me and Kelly were in the middle of all this, I was trying to dance ok in those shoes, and she just grabbed my hand like a leash and led me into the bathroom, into one of the suspicious wet stalls. She shoved me against the wall and started kissing me. Perfect. I had no idea I wanted to be kissed that way but there it was, like a dream remembered. She was pulling my hair, it was long then and she had a fistful of it, pressing my head to the wall. So we went on a date. To Plum Island, a part of Massachusetts I'd never been to, out near New Hampshire. We were in the country and I felt like a kid. The only time I'd ever seen big clumps of trees were on childhood car trips with my grandparents, so it was that plus I had my seatbelt strapped on and Kelly was nearly ten years older than me. She was twenty-eight, and had been to grad school. She was a teacher. Kelly had hair past her butt and teeth that were rotting in her head. It really threw you when she smiled. They were crooked and brown, hanging in her mouth like a giggle. I have a love for women with fucked-up teeth. Working-class girls who couldn't afford dentists. Kelly was so cute. A real lesbian. It was actually intimidating, considering I was well into the second year of blind codependence with Ian. I had managed to stop having sex with him. Sometimes I gave him a hand job when he got cranky, moving my arm in big, jerky spasms like it was an enormous effort. I was trying to make him feel guilty so he'd leave me alone, but it never worked. I just couldn't bring myself to leave him. He rubbed my head at night before we slept. It was a beautiful thing, it made me feel so loved, all warm and sleepy. It was all I could think of when I imagined breaking up with him, those big hands pushing through my hair. It made no sense. At every other moment I was a poorly sealed package of anger and revulsion, dripping and splashing all over him. How was it Ian was able to continue going out with a girl who refused to sleep with him, who made retching noises at the sight of his dick? When we talked about ending it, Ian would cry, and then I would cry. That he loved me felt good, felt certain. The girls and the clubs felt good but good like an amusement park or a waterslide, something too exhilarating to live in. Good like an acid trip, something dangerous and exciting and fun, yes, but you have to come down sometime. You can't walk around tripping all the time. Ian was reality. There were brief, terrifying discussions of marriage. My parents loved Ian, ever since my 20th birthday my mother had taken to reminiscing about her 20th year, how she'd been pregnant, had a baby, named it Michelle. She'd been married two years already when she was 20. As long as Ian and I'd been together. She talked about hope chests, you buy a big wooden chest, and you slowly start to accumulate things for your future — appliances, boxes of fragile and shining christmas bulbs, sheets. All in hope that you'll get married and put the stuff to use. It would be an arty wedding, mine and Ian's. The flower girl would be dressed like a cherub, with angel wings made by Ian. It would be outdoors, in the sun. I was a writer, I could write the vows. This was my life as I drove around in a car with a lesbian, a kid skipping school. At the nightclub she'd been wearing a t-shirt that said BOYS with a big red slash through it. She made it herself. I knew I had to tell her about my double life. I knew I had to be really honest. At another disco a different lesbian had danced with me and later, leaning against the wall talking, I told her I had a boyfriend. She had asked. I wasn't going to lie. She got upset and walked away. She had bought me a drink and I think she wanted her money back.

Plum Island would have been more beautiful in the sun. The sky was grey as mopwater, and it was cold. You didn't want to leave the car. We looked through the window at the trees and all the shrieking birds, mostly seagulls. There was ocean beyond the tall grass, too far to see but you could smell it coming into the car. I couldn't get Ian out of my mind. It was like he was sitting in the backseat with his dick out. It was such a fucked up thing that I was with him, it seemed so messy. I was sitting beside this lesbian and I wanted her to like me. It was quiet in the car, just looking out at the trees, and Kelly started asking me about my life and I plunged in. I told her about this boy, Ian, and how I was going to leave him soon but it was hard because we'd been together so long. It didn't sound so bad, telling it. It didn't seem to faze her. She just nodded and passed me the joint she'd just lit up and asked me about school. I'd finished one semester at Salem State, transferred to UMass-Boston for a second semester and now I was out of money. I thought maybe I'd move to New York. I smoked from the joint and passed it back to her. Kelly was a pothead. She carried this cute little box around with her at all times, cardboard and pasted with pictures and paint. Inside were papers and matches and a pile of pot. She sold it. It was her side job.

Kelly parked the car beside a sandy little trail. She had brought a thermos of red wine, she grabbed it from the car and shut the door. This place is great she said. She was tall and skinny with that remarkable length of hair. The trail led to a ring of boarded up shacks nested with bird families. It used to be a camp, she said, for mentally retarded kids. The kids she taught were mentally retarded. I thought she must be pretty special. We were sitting on the porch of one of the cabins, drinking wine from the thermos. It was pretty spooky. So desolate. It was the perfect stage for an ax murder. The two drunk lesbians move in for the kiss and a masked man rises up behind them with a power tool. We were drinking and smoking pot and chatting and I was wondering if we were going to have sex right there on the porch. I really wanted to. I had had barely any sex with women. I was really anxious to get started. She was wearing a white lace top that her nipples poked through and I was paranoid that I was staring too much and being tacky. I was staring at them when the park ranger walked up. That's why I didn't see him. He was really hostile. He should've been a cop. He didn't at all fit with the idea of park rangers as happy healthy nature-loving people. Protectors of the trees. We weren't allowed to be at the closed up camp. *Didn't you see the sign* he asked. *No trespassing. Can't you read?* He kept asking us if we could read. He was like a horrible father. We followed him back to the car where he took Kelly's license and climbed into his manly ranger truck. Kelly looked really frightened. She was sitting in the car with her face tight and hands shaking. I didn't get why she was so intimidated. He hadn't noticed the wine or the pot so I thought we were set, but it turned out there was something illegal about us, the car not being registered or maybe there was a bunch of parking tickets. If he had found that out he could've taken the car and left us stuck out on Plum Island. All he did was kick us off the land. What an asshole.

Liquor stores in New Hampshire are open on Sundays so that's where we went, over the border in Kelly's illegal vehicle. She seemed kind of like an outlaw now and I was liking her more and more. We got another bottle of wine because she had a bleeding ulcer and wasn't supposed to drink but wine and champagne were ok. She told me about throwing up blood and cabbing to the hospital where she stayed for days with no one to call, no family and no friends. It seized my guts with love. If That Ever

Happens To You Again You Can Call Me. I'll Come. I was kind of drunk but I meant it. We talked about getting tattoos. We were in Seabrook, New Hampshire where there are tattoo parlors everywhere. They're illegal in Massachusetts so everyone in Boston would take road-trips to Seabrook for mass tattooing. All the parlors were run by bikers and if they thought your tattoo idea was stupid they'd charge you more or fuck it up on purpose. That's what I'd heard. Neither of us had money for a tattoo. We drove around and picked lilacs, they had just started blooming. We stopped at a cemetery to eat these amazing sandwiches she'd made for us, cheese and cucumbers and tasty dressing. We drove back to Boston. She was blitzed but drove superb and I was in love.

We went to a disco that night and drank mimosas for free because she was friends with the bartender. We were crawling all over each other and decided to just go home, her home since I still lived with my parents. She had the cutest little apartment in the North End, the Italian section of Boston. It had art and cats and lipstick on the bathroom wall that read You Don't Have To Hate Men To Be A Lesbian/You Don't Have To Be A Lesbian To Hate Men. A little bedroom with a dresser and pillows where we finally had sex. She didn't want me to go down on her which confused me because I thought that's what lesbians did, but she turned out to be very good with her knees. We started seeing each other a lot, at discos, at cafes. I would go to her house and stand in the street shouting Kelly! up at her window because her doorbell was broken. I loved her neighborhood. It was so European, the thin curving streets, it matched the way I felt that summer. Once in her living room I heard festive

74

noises, I leaned out the window to look. Kelly, Come Here! This procession of musicians, a parade right under her window, shining brass instruments and an enormous statue of the virgin carried upon worshipping shoulders. It was like she lived in another country. Across the street was a secret mafia men's club, we watched these hulking creatures in suits sneak in, could see the girlie posters hung on the walls. She would take me shopping in the North End where everything you need has its own special shop, fruit in the fruit shop, cheese in the cheese shop, fish in the wet and stinky fish shop. It was so romantic. We'd take it all back to her apartment where her friend Andrew who hated me always was. I didn't know why he hated me, I thought maybe they had one of those co-dependent dyke/fag relationships and he was jealous. He had a long english face like Ichibod Crane and I referred to him as Ichibod to my friends. He would glare at me and say hello like it was the most arduous task, getting his tongue to form the sound. I didn't care. I was so happy. I was so happy I broke up with Ian. It was disturbingly easy. We were on the phone, I was in Chelsea, in my bedroom which he had recently redecorated for me, covering the spattered fucked-up linoleum with smooth black squares, painting the walls a dense, shineless ebony, nailing up a little ridge called wainscoting for me to line my religious knick-knacks on. He found a gigantic wooden 'I' and when he was finished he nailed it to the wall above my bed. I slept beneath it every night. I stared at it as I spoke into the phone. Ian We Really Shouldn't Go Out Anymore. I was done. And no resistance from Ian. *You're a lesbian,* he said. Uh-Huh. What a cool thing to be. It was like I got to start life all over again. Incidentally, all of Ian's girl-friends were dykes by the time they broke up. He's one of those boys. Anyway, that was the summer that Operation Rescue brought their 'summer of mercy' to Boston and I was out at the clinic every afternoon with signs and chants, hanging out with all my new friends from Queer Nation. They gave me neon stickers that I stuck all over myself, my jacket my bag, my boots. I had all these new queer friends and even a girlfriend. I brought Kelly home to meet my parents. I was shoving it all down their throats with glee. *I was glad to see Kelly has long hair* my mother said.

I was out at a disco, Venus de Milo again. Wednesday night was gay night. The rest of the week it was varying genres of heterosexual. Nathan was there, a big glamour fag who looked like Morrissey with that styling gel swoop on his forehead. I'd known him since Copley and he was glad I'd crossed over to the other side. *Who you likin' girl?* Kelly I said. He knew her too. I've Been Seeing Her. He got this pensive Oscar Wilde look on his face. *Is she still with Andrew?* Andrew? *Yeah, they were together for a while.* Are You Sure? I asked. I Think Andrew's A Fag. *Oh, he is,* Nathan said, *but I don't think he knows it.* Well. Andrew. He was always at Kelly's house and I hadn't slept over since that first night with the leg action. The next afternoon I was in her apartment, sitting in her bedroom. Andrew wasn't there but his clothes were — rows of suits in the closet and a puddle of men's shoes beneath. I hadn't noticed it before. Does Andrew Live Here I asked. *Yeah.* Is Andrew Your Boyfriend? *Yeah. But we don't really have sex.* You Could Have Told Me, I said. I Told You. I Had A

Boyfriend Too. And I had been so upset about it. Here I was thinking she was this big lesbian and she had a boyfriend and didn't even tell me. I was bothered but her face was so upset I let it go. It explained things; how she was so secretive sometimes, nervous with kissing and holding hands. She wasn't out to any of her friends or to her twin brother who lived in the apartment next door. He was this macho irish guy, he was always over buying pot. She came from a big family, poor irish from the projects, she had a string of brothers in and out of jail. She didn't tell any of them. And she didn't break up with Andrew because he had some kind of exotic heart condition and could die any minute.

So Kelly and me were a secret. I was kind of into it. It enhanced the inherent naughtiness of the whole situation and was kind of a turn on. Kelly would rent rooms for us at little Bostonian guest houses, there'd be a key for me at the desk and I'd wait for her there. It was very exciting, lying on the quaint wooden bed, waiting for my forbidden lesbian lover. I was twenty-one, stretched out beneath the window open to the summer. She would arrive at dusk with fruit and wine and pot, we would get nicely buzzed and start kissing. I had plans to be at this meeting, making signs for another abortion rights demonstration. I called and spoke to Liz who would eventually become my lover and fuck up my life. I Can't Make It, I said, I'm At A Hotel Waiting For Kelly. It was such an affair. She showed up with a plastic bag full of scarves which she used to bind my hands behind me. It was hot but silly too, we were stoned and just kept laughing. I was so attracted to her, I had never been so attracted to a person. It seemed to jump right off my chest. We had sex and then sat folded together on the room's only chair, naked and sharing a joint. She was always stoned and it felt appropriate to join her. Clinic defense at six in the morning, we'd walk around the corner away from the cops and light up, walk back and join the chanting. We were activists. It's how you meet other lesbians in Boston. We did condom and needle distribution in the Combat Zone every Friday night and we'd be stoned for that too. Everyone wanted to be the one who gave out the needles because it was illegal. We joined the queer street patrol, the Pynk Panthers, and Kelly would show up for training with her eyes all pink and teary. I thought that was kind of too much. Somewhere it began to bother me that Kelly was not out of the closet. At least when I had a boyfriend I wasn't shy about the fact that I fucked girls too. We went to a party together — Robbie from Queer Nation. Everyone there was a professional queer, they were loud about it, proudly obnoxious, and I started picking up on the vibe that some of the girls liked me. Radical girls who made out on street corners. Kelly was in a black party dress with that shawl of hair around her shoulders, standing quietly in the kitchen. I was ignoring her. It was awful but I felt stifled by her quiet homosexuality. I thought about being with a woman so scared of herself. And closeted queers were our worst enemy. I'd learned that at Queer Nation. My new queer friends thought I should break up with her. I could tell they didn't respect her. I started feeling embarrassed of her, Kelly, this woman who wasn't quite my girlfriend, really, because she wasn't a lesbian, really. I can't remember how I broke up with her, on the phone or in her car while she was driving, something horrible like that. She didn't seem surprised, but then, she was always stoned. After it was over we were together in her car. I was running errands with her. We were at the cemetery so she could visit her father's grave. She had flowers and a bowed head like praying. I was walking around looking at all the statues of beautiful angels and grieving women. Back at the car, Kelly cried. Everywhere was summer.

Get Used To It
Boston, 1991

The summer that I came out I felt indescribably perfect. I had decided not to go to college, to just have fun,
travel, maybe move to New York. Everything seemed possible, like a bubble of options had just burst in my hand.
I was still living at home and being very passive-aggres-
sive about my new lesbianinity, wearing lots of pink triangles and Queer Nation stickers. Saying things like I'm
Off To The Gay Pride Parade as I gleefully skipped out the
door, leaving my parents to deal with their worst fear realized. I was enjoying myself too much to attend to the
more complicated aspects of being a sexual minority. The
spirit of summer, the sun-spirit, the spirit of wine and
warm nights had delivered me to a group of wonderful
loud-mouthed girls who were also unafraid to wear their
queerness as a fashion accessory. One of them, Liz,
became my girlfriend. I had met her at the abortion clinic
on Boyleston Street, I had liked her right away because she
was such an awful bitch to the christians. She was doing
all the things the women from NOW, who had appointed
themselves as leaders of the whole shebang, told you not
to do, like taunt them verbally, call them slimy little ass-
holes, accuse them of molesting their children, slamming
into them and then facetiously apologizing, asking the
women if they've ever experienced orgasm. Simply making
fun of their outfits. Liz and her roommate Teri would cross
the street and in their bras and cut-off shorts stand

among Operation Rescue and the holy statues they'd lugged out of some church, the big full-color posters of drippy red mutilated fetuses. They'd randomly choose one guy and begin to stalk him, follow him through the crowd as he tried to shake them, talking explicitly about how tiny his dick must be and all the perverted things he probably liked to do with it. Then they'd just go ballistic, start screaming at a priest *Motherfucker are you going to raise my baby?! Are you going to tell me what to do with my body?!*, until a cop came over and threatened to arrest them if they didn't go back across the street and resume their positions in front of the clinic. The women from NOW, who thought they owned the entire concept of clinic defense, hated Liz and Teri as much as any christian or cop. They would beg them to behave, saying that they were making our side of the issue look bad for the news cameras. *Fuck you*, Liz spat. After I broke up with Kelly and freed up my time Liz and Teri started asking me to do things with them. They invited me to Teri's parent's summer home, a cottage on a lake somewhere in Connecticut, where they were from. I went with them and another of their friends, Brad. It was clear that they all had had different lives than me. My parents didn't own their own home, never mind a 'summer home', an entire furnished home that sat vacant for most of the year. They also had a boat, for waterskiing on the lake. I couldn't fathom the cost of maintaining all these things. That cottage was furnished better than my regular home. Liz and Teri and Brad and I immediately got drunk on cans of beer, on the wooden pier that stretched out into the lake. Between the nice buzz in the sunshine and the fact that I could tell Liz liked me, I didn't feel too uncomfortable. That night, stoned in the 'rec room' down in the basement, Brad cornered me and said *So you like my friend Liz? You gonna dyke out with her?* Brad was a fag, Teri was straight and at that moment Liz was kind of straight as well, having never slept with a girl before. And I had just assumed that everyone else certainly had more experience than me. Liz had decided she was gay only a couple of days ago, and Teri and Brad seemed really amused by it. Sure, I said, I'll Dyke Out With Her. I am sure I never used the phrase 'Dyke Out' before or since. Me and Brad joined the girls, and Teri and Brad immediately got in a terrific stoned argument and left the room. Liz handed me a freshly packed pipe, I smoked it, choked, handed it back to her and she leaned her body into me, there on the carpeted rec room floor, and we both looked up at the phone sex infomercial on the television screen and cracked up. Liz kissed me. We made out to the affected sexiness of the bikini-clad women on the tv, each with their different erotic personalities. *Let's go to bed*, Liz whispered. We squeezed into the single bottom bunk of the bunk beds in the spare room, and went to work exploring the hidden skin beneath our t-shirts and panties. It's really kind of great to be someone's first girl. I was like a stone from another planet, that amazing, being tumbled around in her palms. When we woke up in the morning Brad and Teri were smirking, and me and Liz were girlfriends.

Becoming girlfriends with Liz did not reduce the exciting possibility of sex with the rest of the girls out there in the world. I don't recall ever discussing monogamy with her, but after all that time swinging with Ian I just assumed it, and Liz went along with me. I think. One woman I had my eye on was Tania, an older woman who promoted clubs in Boston and Provincetown. I had met her months ago at a club, she bought me a drink and I told her I had a boyfriend and she went on to call me *straight girl* for the rest of the night, dancing close to me, grazing my neck with her teeth, saying *not bad for a straight girl*, driving me crazy. I wrote a little story about it, called it *Straight Girl*, put it in a zine I was doing. Now that Ian was compost I thought, Hmmph, Straight Girl, I'll Show Her. Tania was doing a club in a warehouse, it was called G-Spot or Girl Bar, there's one in every major metropolitan city, I think. I was training to be a Pynk Panther, a homo Guardian Angel. I very much believed in the cause but it was more of a social/sexual vehicle. The more experienced Panther girls would use me to demonstrate different self-defence moves, flipping me onto my back and digging a knee into my chest while I panted up at them, completely in love. Tania's club was hosting a benefit for our street patrol, which was exciting but also lousy because we actually had to patrol that night and could only stay at the club for an hour, forbidden to drink. We were encouraged to wear our Panther uniforms so we could leave immediately for the streets and also bring visibility to our cause, but the uniform was unforgivably dorky. An enormous grey t-shirt with a pink triangle and a fist, the brightest fluorescent pink baseball hat that sat on my head like a space-ship. I refused to go to a girl bar looking like such a nerd. I was wanting sex so badly right then, every decision was calculated to increase my chances of getting some. I shoved my uniform into my black army bag and pulled on my hot pink girdle-and-bra ensemble. It was magnificent. The girdle was shiny satin with ribboned garters, the bra was hung with pink tassles, rhinestones, and pearls. Liz wore a pair of scanty shorts and a black bra with a heavy silver hood ornament swinging from the chasm of her cleavage, we both wore tall go-go boots and ran around the club flirting and drinking vodka tonics, telling the patrol leader it was water. When it came time to patrol we were broken-hearted Cinderellas, plastered. You see, the situation was really perfect because I wanted Tania and Liz wanted Tania's girlfriend Christine and they'd been cruising us all night, but by the time we were drunk enough to respond we were being dragged from the ball by the scruff of our necks. Tania intercepted us as we were herded down the stairs. *Awwww*, she said, winding her arms around me and Liz. *Can't you let these two stay?* We made puppy eyes at the stern patrol leader who shook her head and ordered us toward the bathroom and into our uniforms. I dug a copy of my zine from my bag before I left, opened to the *Straight Girl* story. I thrust it at Tania. Here, I said, Read It, Its About You. She looked at the title, offended. She didn't remember me at all. *I'm not a straight girl.* Just Read It! I giggled and ran off to the bathroom.

So here is the first time I ever went to Provincetown. Our mission that weekend, besides fucking up my credit history forever, was to score with Tania and with Christine. Me and Liz were really digging each other, and she was excited to show me this gay haven way out on the spiraling tip of Massachusetts but she only had so much money that weekend so I volunteered my credit card. We got a hotel room in Truro, where the rent is cheaper and the drive to and from P-Town is so nice, past sand dunes and seagrass and those little blue seashacks, a bright

84

sky-colored row, each one named for a flower. Poppy, Honeysuckle, Dandelion. The guy at the hotel was a big fag, I handed him my card, he whizzed it through the little machine and gave it right back to me, dropped it on the counter like it was burning his hands. *Take it take it* he said, shooing his hands at me. *There's a problem, I don't want to have to cut it up.* He called the credit card place and they told him I was maxed. I couldn't believe it. My card was only a few months old. I guess I hadn't been keeping track. Liz paid for the room with basically all the cash we had, and we drove into Provincetown trying to figure out how we could get more. Commercial Street was like a movie set — the strange Provincetown sunlight, people clogging the street on foot and on bikes. The car crawled through them and I hung my head out the window, amazed. It was like some huge event was happening, but that was the event, being there. We parked the car and walked to the pay phones in front of the Library and I was on the horn to my credit card company with a dramatic story about a broken down car, I'm Stranded, Can You Please Up My Limit? *Will 150 be enough* the lady on the phone asked sweetly. Oh That Will Be Just Fine I said, jumping up and down. I hadn't figured out credit cards yet, I felt like people were just giving me money. Liz and I ran down to the big A&P-like liquor store and blew 30 or 40 bucks, big bags of beer, wine, vodka. We ate a lot of fancy seafood and mimosa brunches. We had great trust that Tania and Christine would be in town that weekend, and we were not disappointed. We were at one of the big discos, not the Boatslip but the other one, with the pool in the back. The Crown & Anchor. Tania was out back, sitting at a table by the pool. Look, I poked Liz. It's Tania. *Why don't you go talk to her?* Is Christine Here? Liz shrugged. Is That Her Over There? *I think so.* Are You Going To Talk To Her? Another shrug. She didn't seem so into it. I looked at Tania, alone at her table. Well, Is It OK If I Go Talk To Her? You're Sure? OK, I'll See You Later. I plopped down next to Tania with a bold Hello. She smiled. Tania was older, like 30, and you knew she'd been a dyke forever. She looked like an aging fashion model, and also a little like Martina. Sharp cheekbones, shiny teeth. *I liked your story* she said and bought me a beer. Like last time, only now I wasn't Straight Girl anymore. I knew she would take me home. It's Provincetown, everyone's only there for the weekend so there's no beating around the bush. I didn't see Christine anywhere and thought maybe Liz had gone after her. Me and Tania sat and talked, about her clubs, my zine, then the music was gone and we were all being herded into the street. *Are you going to Spiritus* she asked. It was Bar Rush, when the clubs emptied and queers clustered up and down Commercial Street, not ready to quit partying, howling and dancing in the street, cruising, squeezing into Spiritus for late night pizza and coffee. I Have To Find My Friend, I said. I didn't see Liz anywhere. Would she just leave? I mean, did she just assume I was going home with this woman and split, leaving me stranded in Provincetown without a Good-bye? *Maybe she went to Spiritus* Tania suggested. Yeah, Probably. We pushed our way down Commercial Street. Tania knew a lot of people, she waved and shouted hello to just about every female we passed and I was impressed.

As we neared Spiritus I became less optimistic about finding Liz. There were so many people, it was like the pride parade all over again only more fun and in the dark, a crazy block party. Cops were walking around trying to keep everyone on the sidewalk but it was impossible, there were just too many bodies. I motioned towards Spiritus. I Should Go In And See If She's There. Tania nodded. *Do you want to come home with me?* I smiled. Sure, I said. Amazingly enough, Liz had found a seat inside the crowded pizza place. She was sitting with her brother Jeremy and a few of his roommates, they all lived in Provincetown. Hi I said breathlessly. This was all too exciting for me. Tania Asked Me To Go Home With Her! Liz shrugged. *So go.* Did You Talk To Christine, I asked. Liz shook her head. I Can Tell Tania You Like Her, I said, I Bet She'll Fix You Up. *Don't you dare do that* Liz snapped. I flinched. *That is so fucking kindergarten!* She had this awful, pissed-off look on her face, the one she got when she yelled at the women from NOW. Hey, It's No Big Deal, I said. Just Trying To Help. I paused. Is It Still OK If I Go Home With Her? Liz just stared at me. Her face looked like a rock now, that still. We really had talked very little about this. When back in Boston I had said We Should Pick Them Up, Liz had laughed and said *Yeah...* and that was it. That was enough permission for me, but maybe Liz was just, I don't know, acknowledging a fun idea or something. The boys at the table quietly smoked their hand-rolled cigarettes, listening to me and Liz have this drama. I could have just forgotten the whole thing, sat down with them and began cajoling Liz into being sweet to me again. But there was an older woman out front and she was waiting to take me to bed.

OK, I said awkwardly, Well...How Does This Work? When Will I Meet Back Up With You? Liz shrugged. She had really perfected it, the quick lift-sag of the shoulders. Blank face. Well...OK I'm Sure I'll See You In Town In The Morning. I'll Look For You. I gave Liz a hug and she didn't hug me back. I pushed my way back to the street and scanned for Tania. What if now I'd lost her too and had to spend the night schlepping around Commercial Street. *Michelle*, I heard my name and saw Tania leaning against a storefront, away from the throngs of people. I walked over and she draped a comfortable arm around me. Tania was talking to a short butch woman wearing black clothes and a baseball hat spun backwards on her head. She introduced us. Tania really knew everyone. This woman was a celebrity. Not as much as she is now, since this was before Arsenio Hall and the covers of so many gay magazines, but she was famous enough that I knew who she was and, having a juvenile love of stardom, was impressed. The celebutante was not impressed with me. She shook my hand sternly and looked me up and down. *Are you two going home together* she demanded. I was embarrassed. I nodded. *How old are you* she asked. I felt like I was getting in trouble for something, her voice just reduced me to 12. But I wasn't 12. I'm 21 I told her and the word child registered in her eyes. *Are you a lesbian?* I nodded. *When was the last time you slept with a boy?* Two Months Ago, I said. She was just drilling me. I have no idea why. If this occurred now I would surely tell her to fuck off, but I was so overwhelmed — the older woman beside me who was taking me home for sex, the bitchy famous person, the screaming queens all around us and, some-

88

where, my grouchy girlfriend. *Did you use a condom,* continued the superstar. I said yes. It was a lie, but by now I knew I was under attack. *Have you been tested for HIV.* I can't remember what I said. I hadn't. It was so weird. For Tania's sake I did not want to lie, but I resented this famous stranger's attempts to extract my sexual history so she could judge it. Tania was just quiet. Eventually the famous lesbian ignored me. She turned to Tania and it was like I wasn't even there. What was she talking about, sex. *I just want to find a girl who'll fuck me up the ass* she was saying. Then she went away. I saw her the next summer, again in Provincetown. By then me and Liz were psychotically feminist and we got in a big fight with Miss Fame right on Commercial Street, for comments she made about Hillary Clinton at the March on Washington. It was pretty ridiculous. Mostly it was Liz needing to start trouble and me not knowing what to do, the basic theme to develop in our relationship. The superstar was with this gang of athletic butchy girls in a lot of makeup. They were making fun of Liz's dreadlocks. *Nice haaaair* they whined at us in their dreadful accents. And to bring it right up to the present, I actually saw this famous lesbian last week in a cafe. She had a limo double-parked out front and the chauffeur was eating at a separate table. And then that night her and her friends showed up at this divey dyke bar, a real hole, and they were all dressed up in expensive clothes — a movie director, a magazine person, and the hated superstar. They were totally slumming. When they left I rushed to their table and took all their half-empty drinks back to my friends. We drank them. Rum and cokes.

So back to Tania. *Do you want to take a walk* she asked. We strolled down Commercial Street, away from the crowd and the bars from which they poured. We were walking past quaint little houses, wood painted in faded pastels, gardens in the front, roses and vines of honey-suckle. Every now and then we'd pass an alley that ran down to the ocean and there'd be a silhouetted figure, male, leaning against the wall, thumbs hooked through belt loops. I pointed him out to Tania. *Oh,* she waved her hand, *they'll be out here til the sun comes up.* We walked to the end of Commercial Street, we were leaning against a wooden fence and beyond it was a marsh, swampy green grass and shiny spots of water. Tania pushed me up against the fence and went for my neck, not with her lips but with her teeth. She dug them in hard and I gasped with pleasure and surprise. Her fingertips were just as rough, finding my nipples and squeezing them tightly. I was shocked. You'd think someone would ask if it was ok before they started chomping and pinching on you, I mean what if you didn't like that, what a thing to assume. I threw back my head and offered my neck like a slab of meat to a lion. I rubbed my body up against her the way I did that night in the club, when she whispered *not bad for a straight girl.* I wasn't a straight girl. I shot a moan into her ear and she moaned right back, took my hand and said *let's go to my house.*

Tania's house was off Commercial Street, right around the corner from Spiritus, where the crowd had thinned but not disappeared. A group of fags were sitting on the porch next door, drunk and talking loud. *I'm not moving to San Francisco,* one proclaimed. *It's a conspiracy, they want us all in one place so they can bomb it.* The inside of Tania's house was dark and lit with fancy blue lights. It looked like one of her clubs. The bathroom's over there if you need it she said, pointing into the darkness. I navigated my way towards it, dragging my hands across the wall til I hit the door. There was toothpaste lying on the sink, I squeezed some on my finger and tried to brush my teeth. The doorknob rattled. One Minute I gurgled flirtatiously. I opened the door not to Tania, but to her roommate, a woman who stared at me with obvious disapproval and entered the bathroom without a hello. What was it with these women? What a bunch of bitches they all were. I stumbled back to Tania's room. Her house was actually very nice, large rooms with wood floors and lots of windows. The simple fact that Tania lived in an apartment and not one of the skanky rooming houses that everyone else in P-town existed in made me think she probably had money. She looked like she came from money, the way she spoke and carried herself. Aristocratic. Tania shut off the overhead light as I entered the bedroom. She switched on more blue lights and again I felt like I was inside a disco. I was on my back on the bed and Tania was on top of me. I didn't realize how drunk I was until I was lying down with my head spinning. Tania was tugging off my jeans and gnawing at my neck. I raised my hips to help her along and tried to breathe the spins away. This part is murky but I do remember her hand inside me, not her entire hand but certainly more of her hand than of any other hand ever before inside me. I couldn't decide if I liked it. Partly it felt like an examination. She was touching areas previously only touched by doctors. I was waiting for it to hurt, it seemed so much, but it didn't so I tried to relax my muscles and get more into it. Then Tania hit a spot that made me feel like I was going to pee, or that I was peeing, I couldn't figure out which and I was horrified because what if I was peeing on her? And if it felt like that, was she doing something bad, was her hand in a place it shouldn't be? Tania's hands were at her own pelvic level and she was bucking her hips into them, pushing them deeper into me. She was really into it; I think she was pretending her hands were a dick. A strap-on would've been easier, but then I wouldn't have gotten that strange peeing sensation that I now know is the precursor to a g-spot orgasm, something I did not have because I was too worried about wetting the bed. But at least I know what they're talking about when I read about it in sex books.

OK, the sun came into Tania's window and cracked my eyes like an egg. I looked around the foreign room and the first, most primal part of my brain, the scent-propelled animal brain, awoke and responded with panic to the unfamiliar form that was curled completely around me, lying half on my back. This place of instinct, the lizard-brain, intuited that it was not the rounder, softer form it usually awoke to, and so the rest of the brain perked up and the face of Liz flashed clearly in my head and I thought Fuck. Fuck fuck fuck fuck. What time was it? What if we'd slept all day and the sun was on its way back down and Liz was on her way back to Boston. Could I just slip out of Tania's house, was that inexcusably rude or did people expect and maybe prefer that from one-night-stands. It was agonizing to lie there beneath Tania's sleeping, oblivious weight. The panic came in thin streams that trickled electricity down my chest, I needed to be up and moving, crawling around Commercial Street in search of my girlfriend. My nose was stuffy and each time I exhaled it squeaked and it was really annoying and I couldn't make it stop. I was sniffing like crazy, rubbing and itching it, and through this activity I eventually woke Tania up and convinced her to stay up, though she looked like she could've used another hour or two in the sack. We got out of bed, into some clothes and left the house. My velvet top was stale and smoky from the night before but Tania was clean and shiny. I was calming myself down by visualizing worst-case-scenarios and living through them. What was the worst that could happen? I visualized hitchhiking back to the hotel in Truro. People hitchhiked all the time in Cape Cod, I could find a ride with a woman or a queer. I could probably hitch all the way back to Boston if I needed to. Tania wanted to buy me breakfast and that was nice because I had forgot to get actual cash from Liz before I ran out on her and had in my pocket about 3 dollars and a spent credit card. We went to this cute restaurant and sat out on the patio, I ordered coffee and a little bowl of fruit and listened to Tania talk about her life. She was into marketing. She had gone to school for it, graduate school even, and she talked about different experiences she had with it and what she wanted to do with it in the future and I was completely lost, like, what the fuck is marketing? It sounded incredibly boring. I asked her to explain it, I think it had to do with advertising, it certainly was corporate and I couldn't relate at all. I am an enemy of advertising, of corporations, I am an enemy of the entire notion of careers and as Tania continued to speak I realized I was probably an enemy of Tania. She told me about her recent ex-girlfriend and her ex-girlfriend's career and I cursed the lack of thought that had thrown me into this awful situation. I mentioned Liz and my concern about finding her, carefully masking both my panic and the fact that Liz was my girlfriend. I guess I could've just been honest and it wouldn't have been a big deal. Girls with girlfriends are always up and fucking other girls but I was new to this idea and couldn't help but feel sneaky. And Liz had hated that I had gone home with her, Corporate Tania, the career woman. Easily ignored in the drunken darkness of my night on the town, I could not escape it in the clear sunlight of Sunday morning. Was I an asshole or what. What was I doing eating a bowl of fruit with this woman who was not my girlfriend, who was in fact a capitalist, a perpetuator of the system that me and my true love were engaged in noble battle against. Luckily the capitalist had a car. It was a crappy car, a big old boat on wheels, not the car of a woman ascending the corporate ladder, but it was a car and it worked and it drove me out of Provincetown. The romantic ride past ocean and sand. Tania, feeling generous, took the scenic route and pointed out to me the different Cape Cod landscapes, offered to take me on a hike through the dunes. Liz came up again; the intense guilt I was feeling compelled me to confess as if Tania could absolve me but of course that was foolish so I told another lie, I said Liz was a good friend but she kind of had a crush on me and was maybe upset that I had gone home with someone. Tania saw through it immediately, I watched the situation register in her face and she said *oh is that what's going on, why didn't you say that* and I rushed to cover it up with additional lies but she was quiet the rest of the drive to the hotel. And then Liz wasn't there. My heart sank when I saw the empty parking space outside our bungalow, but the door was cracked open so I hopped out of the car and flung myself into the room. It was dark, there were dark masses on the floor that stirred and rose as I entered. Boys, Liz's brother Jeremy and his roommates. Here and there around the room were the bottles I'd charged at the liquor store, empty. Where's Liz, I demanded, and her brother squinted at me through the sleep in his face. *I don't know* he said groggily. I figured he probably thought I was a real jerk. Did She Go Into Town, Did She Go To The Beach? I was desperate. Behind me, Tania's car idled in the sun. *I think she went to the beach* one of the roommates piped up. I ran back to the car. Umm... I Think She Went To The Beach. I Guess I'll Wait Here For Her. *Which beach* asked Tania. I told her the name, she was impressed. It was the nicest beach on Cape Cod; an enormous sand dune, rust-colored and glinting, ran down the length of it. It was private, you could only go there if you owned property in Truro, the way Liz's wealthy parents did. They owned a vacant lot somewhere in town. We got in a vicious fight once, on the sweet green road that led to the water, because I thought that rule was classist. Liz said it was for the good of the beach, people from out of town wouldn't respect it and they'd walk on the dunes and cause erosion but that was pure bunk because the Truro people were always running up the dune, chasing their frisbees or just showing off. Anyway, Tania drove me to the beach. I guess she had nothing to do that day. I didn't know how to say good-bye to her when we finally arrived. I Had Fun. Thanks A Lot For Everything. *Sure.*

Maybe I'll see you at my club. We hugged. I ran down the big sand dune and dropped onto the beach. There I was. What a magnificent landscape for my panic. The infinite ocean, cresting and crashing like the fear in my belly. Liz always plopped her blanket far down on the beach, away from the people so she could take off her clothes. I rushed through the sand, too impatient to stop and pull off my boots even though their weight on the soft terrain only slowed me down, like a dream where a killer chases you quickly but you're in slow motion. For the longest time the beach before me was empty, a virtual desert despite the waves that crawled forward. Then there was a spot, a thing, far down the shore. It could've been anything, a log, an old bucket dredged up by the tides, but it was Liz naked on hands and knees, carefully constructing a sandcastle. What a sight I must have been, stumbling up in last night's clubwear, velvet bodysuit, jeans and boots, leather jacket slung over my shoulder. Hi I said, collapsing onto the blanket. *Hi* she said. She looked at me as one would any apparition. *How did you get here?* Tania, I said. *How was that* she asked. That Was A Nightmare I said, and it felt true. It Was Awful. Liz smiled. *Why was it awful?* Well... I Could've Been With You. *I came here and looked at the moon* Liz said. That sounded so nice. Sitting on the beach, looking at the moon with my girlfriend. I'm Sorry I said. She shrugged and planted a garden of sea grass outside the castle door. I Was So Worried, I said, pulling off my clothes. I Thought Maybe You Went Back To Boston. *I almost did*, she said, *I really thought about it.* I watched her crawl around the sand. What was my connection to her. She was this person, what did it mean. Can I Help You With Your Castle?

No she said. I stood up and started down the empty shore. I collected every piece of trash I came upon, a rusted aerosol can, straws, nuggets of styrofoam, a Snickers wrapper. I built my own empire, the Darth Vader of sand castles, the antithesis of Liz's little world of seashells and fragile, sun-bleached crab parts. *What are you doing* she demanded as I fastened the candy wrapper to the straw, creating a flag for my nation. This Is My Kingdom, I said. I Think We're At War.

* ★ *

Sitting around in Liz's beautiful apartment crowded with coffee and lazy cats and the furniture that Teri was ruining because she didn't know how to take care of anything. The previous week her boyfriend rode his motorcycle in the rain and left wet pants on the lamp til they caught fire and dropped burning onto that nice leather chair. Liz got up early to pee and said *Look Michelle, there's a cloud in the house* in the sweetest sleepy voice, like she was walking her dream to the bathroom. Really it was smoke and Liz woke up Teri and the boyfriend and got back into bed while they put it out. We pushed clothes along the bedroom door to keep out the burning smell. It all came from the same flaw in her personality — Teri couldn't keep things nice and her boyfriends were always stupid. That's what Liz was saying. Sitting around their apartment with sun coming in through the porch and splashing onto the wood floor where the cats swam orange and grey in the light. I always thought that some people had money and some people didn't and I never asked questions of the ones who did because I figured it was something I just wouldn't understand. Thick blue glasses that held coffee, an antique sewing table with rows of little drawers like secrets, I didn't want to know their history; I just touched them and accepted that they were there. The bathroom was filled with things to put on your skin, mango things and avocado things, it was like Liz and Teri were from another country and this was the stuff of their culture.

Actually they were whores. I was the last to know. It makes sense that Liz didn't tell me right away. In the Queer Nation/Pynk Panthers/R2N2 feminista baby dyke circle we all suddenly found ourselves a part of, sex work was less of a personal reality than it was another issue to bat around and debate. A lot of girls thought it sucked. For the usual reasons — it fed sexism, fed rape even, things that we were engaged in earnest battle against. I think I pretty much agreed with that, but I was never angry at the women who did it. I figured they were mostly like the street whores and strippers my Uncle Charlie dated and married. Poor women, sweet but ignorant of the larger stage of misogyny they were dancing on. Eating dinner at Peking On The Prudential — where I first discovered the delicious little dumplings that were pot stickers, called Peking Ravioli there — all the activist girls were talking about Abby who had auditioned a few nights ago at the Naked I. I guess you go in and do a little dance up on the stage, take your clothes off or whatever, and the manager — who I imagined to be a chain-smoking sleazeball — would watch you and rate you, all the while getting off on it and you weren't even getting paid yet. He must audition tons of girls just for the personal show. But Abby did good, and they offered her a job and she thought she might take it. *She doesn't need to*, Nicki was saying. She was sort of the Head Activist, had been doing it longer and more of it than any of us. *There are plenty of other ways to make money. She just likes getting attention from men. And then she tries to be political, you can't have it both ways.* Abby was bisexual. Nicki saw this as not only a problem, but the essential problem that led her into the peepshow. I remember Liz stuck up for her. So did Lara and Kate, the two girls who me and Liz had formed the closest friendship with. And they all yelled at me later for not sticking up for Abby too. Well I Didn't Chime In Against Her, I said defensively. I was just listening, trying to figure it all out. How could I have known Liz was a prostitute? I mean, she had all that money, but I figured she just had it. You know, from Connecticut. Most people had more than me and my family; it wasn't all that interesting. There were many times when I couldn't be with her, times she told me she needed to write, or babysit for a couple hours, or visit one-on-one with some friends. It seemed to be a good way not to be co-dependent, this time apart. I didn't want to be a clingy girlfriend, and besides, I liked moving around, doing my own things, knowing that somewhere out there was a girl and she was my girlfriend. Well my girlfriend was out there on her couch, waiting for calls to come through on her phone. And often Lara and Kate were there with her, all of them hanging out watching videos, crank calling Jerry Falwell's 800 number, having political discussions. Liz finally told me because the three of them missed me on those nights. Her voice was so heavy the words split as they left her mouth. I thought she was going to tell me she had cancer, or AIDS, and my blood slowed down in anticipation of the impact. When she told me she was a prostitute I just laughed.

Then I was excited. I wanted to know all about it. My favorite books were always the books about prostitutes, and junkies, criminals, runaways. I had always wanted to exist among them, and here was Liz. And not just Liz, but Teri too, and occasionally Brad. You Must Have The Best Stories, I said, and then I got to hear them. Liz and Teri, regally regaling us with the most sordid tales, all these stupid men and the men *were* stupid, the joke was clearly on them and not on Liz. Liz was tough, and fearless, and smart. All the things a whore should be. Uncle Charlie's girlfriends had all been tough, but few poor women aren't. I could only imagine they'd have to be fearless to do what they did, but I never thought they were very smart. I could have been wrong. Liz seemed to grow before me with this new information, taking on the stature of myth, and I was thrilled to be involved in her secret. Tell me, what is the opposite of slumming? Vacationing? I was on vacation. I was naked on the couch or maybe in Liz's robe, the deep red one that felt nice and smelled like the bathroom. I wore it because it went with the apartment. Maybe I was reading a book, feminist theory. All the books were feminist theory or else they were the science fiction and trashy pulp that Teri read. Another personality flaw. Also she drank too much and was messy. Liz was hating Teri all that morning over coffee. It was like they were sisters, their relationship was so dysfunctional. Liz was next to me on the couch and probably she was naked. She had a tattoo on her shoulder that she was very conceited about, a naked woman that was really a tree, with a snake twining up her roots to chomp on her nipple. Once someone put an ad in the gay personals to find the woman with that very tattoo. People were always

100

asking her what it meant and that drove her crazy. She had another one, on her ankle, a band of flowers that were faded because she laid on the beach right after she got it. So Liz was on the couch naked except for the tattoos, complaining about Teri and drinking coffee she fixed sweet and creamy. She told me we were going to Lara and Kate's house that night to all have sex together. Really? I was delighted. I knew that once I became a lesbian things like this would start happening to me. We'd all joked about it for so long, never knowing who was more joking and who was more serious. Lara and Kate were always telling me how cute I was. At a nightclub once I got up from the table to talk to a friend and they started hollering about how great my ass was. I was wearing gold rubber short-shorts designed to make anyone's ass look like Wonder Woman's.

Liz wanted to sleep with Kate who was young and looked like a boy or a rabbit, and I wanted to do it with Lara, tall and loud with a gap between her teeth. We finished the coffee and took showers, rubbed sweet stinky things on our skin and did what, I don't know, drove around in the car maybe, ran errands, ate lunch. Then it was night and we had wine, we were in Beacon Hill where Lara and Kate were living, in one of the brick buildings that walled the narrow streets, we were ringing their bell, climbing their stairs. They rented the attic room of an apartment two fags lived in, I don't remember their names but they were weird. One was short and dark and looked like a maniac — I think it was his eyes. He was intense, alcoholic, Lara and Kate were afraid of him because he'd get too drunk and become violent and break things. It was like he was a terrorist or something.

I remember being at a party and both of us were drunk and he talked wildly about blowing things up and I felt like he would really do it. He wasn't an activist. Activists never blow things up even though they want to, because their hearts are too big and tender. That's why they're activists. This guy was just crazy. The other guy was slender, quiet and I had a hard time believing he was gay because his hair was long and he looked like a hippie. He was a real potsmoker but his current boyfriend didn't like it so he would have to hide to get stoned and then pretend he was sober, which I imagined would make you really paranoid. He was a masseuse. Liz was always trying to get him to rub her feet. And these guys were slobs. They weren't home that night but there was food rotting on the kitchen table and the whole place smelled terrible. Liz, who was very fastidious, asked Lara how she could live in a place with rotting food on the table and Lara just shrugged and said it was their house, the boys. It's like they were boarders.

Lara and Kate had just left this progressive college somewhere north where it never gets warm, the kind of school where you put paint on your body and dance naked for your final project and you get an A. It was very expensive and they couldn't afford it anymore so they were living in this attic in Beacon Hill trying to figure out what to do with their lives. Lara owed something like forty thousand dollars in loans. She probably still does. Their attic room was big with walls that sloped down and formed triangles. They had a giant futon wedged beneath one of the slants and the whole place seemed like a clubhouse. I felt giddy there, like we were kids doing something sneaky. Like there were parents somewhere looking for us. It was summer then and that attic was so hot and the one square window wouldn't open so we took our shirts off cause we were dykes and could do that. We were sitting around with no shirts on, all sweaty eating pizza and drinking so much wine. They had this siamese cat that was very nervous and shit everywhere so the boys made them keep it in the attic, though I don't know why since they lived like such pigs. After a while you didn't even notice the stench; your nose got used to it.

Lara was playing a tape of old music, Pat Benatar and Eddy Grant and I kept laughing, saying Oh My God I Remember This Song! and she'd smile and turn it up. We were talking and talking and getting drunk off the wine, talking about abuse probably because Liz had been raped twice and talked about it constantly, even though she'd never been raped really, it was all just a lie, but she didn't admit that until later so when she talked about it, it was this solemn sacred thing and we felt her pain and the pain of all women and she was like this catholic saint who had survived terrible torture and now was holy. Then we were really drunk, Liz and Kate were trying to get me and Lara to dance for them like they were sailors or something, sitting propped against the wall and me and Lara were on the rug giggling and falling over each other. I think Lara was maybe going to do it but it seemed silly so we just all fell into sex. Lara was kissing Liz and exclaiming *I'm kissing Liz!* and laughing, like it was this funny thing she'd wanted to do for a long time. Me and Kate were watching them and then we started kissing too and then no one had clothes on and we were all over the futon, spilling onto the rug.

We became paired off Liz-Lara, Michelle-Kate, which wasn't the original plan but I suddenly felt all this electric stuff about Kate. It was all that dark red blur from the wine, we were so drunk and sweaty in that hot room and Kate was putting all these fingers into me and moving them like crazy and no one had ever done that to me before and it was making me fly right out of my skin. What Are You Doing I remember asking. How In The World Are You Doing That. Do It Again. She made me say please. She made me say it three or four times. Her fingers lingered in my doorway as I repeated myself, that one little word coming out in a whisper. Then a sudden, violent push inside and my body was buckling like one receiving a shock treatment. Liz and Lara were a mound on the other side of the room doing who knows what. I was really liking Kate. She was younger than me, something like 18 but right then she seemed about 30, knowing how to do that with her hand. Liz had only slid a shy finger into that place, then took it right out, not quite knowing what to do. It's like we thought it was male. Lesbians were all about clits. Somehow Kate and I ended up in the hallway and I was having her do that again, my back against the rickety railing that would have sent me down the stairs had it snapped. Kate was such a dyke. She had a girlfriend when she was 13, that really impressed me. I was in love with Billy Idol when I was 13.

At some point we were back in the room on the bed and Lara ran up naked with cheeks bulging and spit huge globs of honey all over us. It was the most beautiful thing, the honey leaving her mouth, it was so dark you could hardly see it but it shone. She was like a big exotic bug, those insects that spit weird liquids on their mates and prey. Once on our bodies the honey was disgusting. It wouldn't come off no matter how many mouths dug at it. It mixed with sweat and cunt and tasted strange. I went to the shower with Kate to wash it off. The bathroom was small and stunk like boy pee, so cramped you had to sit sideways with your legs out the door to use the toilet. We were in the shower for so long, just kissing and being wet. I was trying not to let my body touch the shower curtain which was grey and slimy. It was odd how before I didn't feel anything great about Kate and now I was crazy about her. It happened that quickly. The water went from warm to cold and we stayed there being delirious until there was a rumbling and the curtain flew back and Lara was there being a bug again, spitting mouthfuls of wine at us. Liz was right behind her. They were annoyed that we were being a couple. We left the shower and went back to the room and I was feeling like I neglected Liz so I brought my face down to her cunt but it was too late, she was falling asleep. I didn't realize this, I thought she was in some kind of sex haze. *Michelle, I'm falling asleep* she said. I went back to Kate and smoked Camels with her. I had this crush now. We slept beside each other but really we were all beside each other with sweaty arms and legs everywhere. I didn't know who was who and I thought that was pretty cool.

Me and Kate went on a date. How awkward. She and Lara were having all these problems and then she wanted to go on a date with me. Actually, I asked her. It was during queer street patrol, we were marching around this really hostile neighborhood in Cambridge in our dorky pink baseball hats and t-shirts, and Kate was in front of me. I kept staring at the back of her head, and she'd turn around and peek at me. So I asked her out. Lara said fine, she didn't mind and went to have sex with this guy that liked her. Liz just thought it was amusing. Maybe even ridiculous. She thought Kate was very young. She'd say things like *Wait til you get older* and Kate would be furious. It was ageist. Also, it was discussed that Kate wasn't comfortable being a woman because she read only male writers and philosophers and wouldn't wear lacy bras for Lara. Liz and I slept with Kate one more time before the big date and there was a lot of tension and Liz said she didn't want it to happen again. I was actually relieved, threeways always make me nervous. I get obsessed with making sure everyone's feeling included.

For our date I took Kate to this place I loved, it was an old fire escape that climbed up the side of a church and hung over a small cemetery. Vines grew up the side until you could barely see the stone and it was very beautiful. You could dangle your feet off the edge and scare yourself. What If There's An Earthquake? *Boston doesn't get earthquakes!* Yeah, But What If One Happens? We had to climb a couple fences to get to this place, and sneak across the patio of a fancy french restaurant. We brought wine again, and cigarettes, and we talked about things like schizophrenia as a mystical experience and all her male poets and philosophers and how more than being a woman or gay it was all about class. We made out, leaning into the wall, our faces sunk in the vines. Her voice when she asked to kiss me gave me shivers. Finally drunk, we managed to scale the fences and headed through the Boston Common, up Beacon Hill to her apartment. The fags were asleep and Lara was with that boy. Kate was talking in this vague way about obsession, like she got obsessed with people or something but it was all very murky and I didn't probe. We slept together again but it felt weird, even Kate's finger trick couldn't jolt away the fact that I was in Lara's bed. Thoughts of Liz home alone and Lara with that boy and what were we all doing exactly. Lara later said she had come home and seen the empty wine bottle and the messy bed and said *oh Kate and Michelle had their date.* And then they were fighting, Lara and Kate, things getting ugly and Lara telling her *You're going to read about this later in one of her 'zines* and me feeling offended and saying I Wouldn't Do That but here I am. Pages of poems from Kate, all kinds of angst and internal pain and one real sweet one that ended *I'll scratch my left eyebrow for you anyday* which was a reference to a hand signal used by fags in a jail somewhere to mean I love you. And then it stopped. I don't remember how. It was so hot that summer and I was drunk. Later Liz would say remember when you were dating Kate and laugh, like it was a joke.

Liz's brother was teasing her about being a whore. He wasn't serious, he had no idea that Liz was a whore. Everyone thought she was a nanny or did catering or something. She had a problem keeping her stories straight but no one seemed to notice. I bet it was because her parents were so rich, everyone knew that, so it was just accepted that Liz had lots of money yet never seemed to work. And she was so generous, why ask questions. The pot we were smoking that afternoon was hers, the greenest, sweetest-smelling pot I'd ever smoked. It almost tasted like sage. Liz was sitting on the carpet, shoulders hunched over the bong, pulling up smoke with her lungs. Jeremy was laughing at her. *First you'll sell your CDs, then your jewelry, before you know it you'll be out on the street, you'll be a pot whore.* Liz pulled herself off the bong and looked at me, cheeks puffed like a big stoned frog. *Did you know you were getting involved with an addict* he asked me, still joking. Jeremy was getting it all right and he didn't even know it. Liz blew out the smoke and said *yeah, I'll have her turning tricks for me soon* and I laughed and drank some beer. The room was thick with alcohol breath and old smoke and the things me and Liz weren't saying.

We were visiting Jeremy at his place in Provincetown. We were there nearly every weekend that summer. Liz made so much money she'd bring us out of the city and set us up by the ocean, eating lobster like two rich daughters. Liz was wanting to come out about her true profession, and had planned to start that weekend by telling her brother Jeremy. It was the right thing to do. We were honest righteous women and knew that people only lie about the things they're ashamed of. Liz wasn't ashamed. She was making good money and taking it easy. I'd come home from my new job at the middle-eastern cafe, feet sore, hungry because my cheap boss wouldn't let me eat for free, not even the hummus, there'd be grease on my shirt and I'd stink of schwarma and Liz would smile with all the happiness of not being me and say *I'd rather suck a big dick for a hundred dollars and be done with it.* She was so smart and brave. After she told Jeremy she would tell all her friends and then she'd tell her parents and after that she'd be lecturing at universities across the country about being a feminist prostitute and how it just makes sense. Liz had big plans. We'd get really stoned and talk about how we were the smartest women who really got what was going on in this world, we were going to write books about it and get famous. After the summer. Summer was about lying lazy at the beach and trips into the country, so high the roadside trees turned into a great green smear and my skull felt like a vise on my brain.

That weekend we were sleeping on the floor in Jeremy's filthy apartment. The place stunk of grease and musty bodies and none of the bedrooms had doors, only faded sheets that hung like sad capes in the doorway. Jeremy shared the apartment with four or five other kids and the only one of them who held a job was Harold who worked part time at an ice cream shop and consequently smelled like a lactating cow. They looked alike, Jeremy and Harold, with long blonde hair they never washed, callused bare feet and jeans worn soft and dirty. They were best friends and had just spent the past six months traveling the country in Steven's sports car, getting gas vouchers from the Salvation Army and food stamps in every other state. They were in Provincetown for the summer and the idea was for Jeremy to teach Harold photography and for Harold to teach Jeremy to fix cars. So far they'd been spending their days getting wasted and nights passed out together on the mattress they shared at the back of the house. We thought they were adorable. *They love each other so much*, Liz would say, *they're just like lovers!* Being newly gay we wanted everyone else to be gay too. We were still very excited about the whole thing, my boots were papered with Queer Nation stickers and Liz's baseball hat read Dyke. Everything was very fresh and blissful except Liz still liked boys a little. Very little. Just every now and then. She liked Dmitri, the greek boy who worked at a clothing store on Commercial Street. He would check us out whenever he walked by and it gave Liz a thrill. He was exactly the type of boy I liked in high school, tall and lanky with no hair on his body but tons on his head, all these thick black curls spinning down his back. Dark eyes and tight jeans. He was sitting on Liz's mind heavy that weekend. We'd be on the patio of a restaurant slurping steamers and she'd see him pass by in a thick throng of tourists. *There he is!* She gulped her wine. *We could fuck him* she said. Do You Think So? She rolled her eyes and gulped more wine. *We can fuck anyone we want to. Who wouldn't want to fuck us?* Now, this is why I was in love with Liz. She was completely in love with herself. I'd never seen anything like it. All the girls I'd ever been around had been successfully schooled in the feminine art of self-deprecation called Modesty. Then came Liz, acting like the world wanted to buy her dinner. I was enchanted. Soon I started to act like that too, and before I knew it I believed it. We moved through that summer like a couple of goddesses down from the mountain for some fun in the slums. After some wine and a joint I wanted to fuck Dmitri too, simply because I realized I could. I had never pursued a boy for sex before, not even while attempting to be straight. Aside from the basic lack of attraction there was a feeling of intimidation. Their bodies, the way they held themselves with subtle arrogance. It had always felt threatening to me, but realizing that I didn't have any desire to fuck them stripped them of all their power. They didn't scare me. Now that I was a fearless dyke I could fuck any boy I wanted. It seemed to make sense. Except the thought of fucking Dmitri didn't move me. I was with Liz, walking down dark Commercial Street, joints cupped in our palms. It was obvious that whether or not we fucked Dmitri hinged on my decision. I had never had sex with someone I felt inherently superior to. That could be interesting. What If We Tied Him Up I suggested. *That's hot,* Liz said. *We need rope, though.* I thought of Dmitri with his skinny arms stretched up behind him and all that hair in his face. He looked like such a girl. Yeah, Let's Do It I said. It'll Be An Experience. I was very into having Experiences. We walked over to the store he worked at and sat down on the curb across the street. Dmitri was closing up, bringing racks of clothes inside and shutting off the lights. He kept turning in our direction but I couldn't tell if he was looking at us because he was wearing sunglasses. He Thinks He's Really Cool I said and Liz chuckled. I felt great right then, sitting in the street with the night pulled open like a piece of fruit. The moon was out and the air was cold enough to roll our bare legs with goosebumps. Liz called out to Dmitri and he came right over, as if he had been expecting it. *Do you want to get stoned* she asked. *Do you want to come to a hotel with us so we can tie you up?* Dmitri said *sure.* He didn't even flinch. He had a slow wide smile that was gorgeous and I thought about all my straight girlfriends I could fix him up with.

Dmitri's father owned a hotel on the beach and that's where we went. Dmitri sat in the back of Liz's car smoking Marlboros and clearing his throat. None of us knew what to say. Liz looked like she just swallowed herself whole and liked the way she tasted. Her eyes were squinty with pot and it made her look evil in a sexy kind of way. She didn't look nervous at all. Now that we had the living breathing man that was Dmitri in our car, I was much less sure of this adventure. I thought maybe I should be a little more stoned. The pipe in the glove box was spent and all the fresh weed was snug in Liz's pocket. I hung my arm out the window and watched the dark ocean pass. I tried not to fidget.

Liz pulled the car into the hotel driveway and Dmitri ran inside to get us a key, leaving Liz and I alone together listening to k.d. lang on the car stereo. She lifted her ass off the seat and dug the plastic bag of pot from her back pocket. My nervousness was resting plainly on my face and Liz was staring at me, picking through the sticky green with her fingers. *Are you sure you want to do this* she asked. *We can just take off* she said *we can turn around and go.* It was my out and I turned it down. I didn't want to be a chicken. I didn't want Liz to be the fearless and desirable one and me to be the dumb little baby. And I didn't ever want to be afraid of anything, especially a boy. Hurry Up With That, I said. Liz was slow with the pot, carefully picking out the seeds and crumbling the rest into the bowl. *He's going to have a huge dick* she said, and my stomach lurched. How Do You Know That? *He's greek,* she said. *I'll bet you anything it's giant.* She passed me the pipe and I quickly dipped a flame into it. *Really,* Liz insisted, *if you want to leave we can.* I was beginning to wonder if maybe she didn't want to go through with it either and was hoping I'd back us out of it. Fuck that. She didn't want to be chicken and neither did I. Here Comes Dmitri I said and slammed myself out of the car.

Liz was very proud of her ability to maneuver free stuff out of men — money and gifts from her tricks, compliments and alcohol in bars. She was excited that we had gotten ourselves a free beachfront hotel room in Provincetown, where the guest inns could get pretty expensive. But Dmitri's dad's place was more like the nearby Holiday Inn than the quaint houses on Commercial Street with rosebush gardens and wrought iron fences. It had two fat beds with ugly pastel blankets, a TV propped on the nightstand and an old rotary dial phone. A simple white bathroom with a shower. Dmitri plopped down on one of the beds and lit up a cigarette, his long denim legs cutting across the carpet. His smile made me think he was probably a very nice person. He was about to become the third boy I had ever had sex with, and I didn't even know his last name. He cleared his throat some more and started telling us how he was going into Boston later that week with all his greek relatives. They were going to a greek bar where they broke plates on the floor and danced and maybe we would like to go with him. Liz said *sure* with a big smile on her face and I felt uneasy and wanted to remind her that we generally didn't like men. We passed around pot and cigarettes, filling up the stale air-conditioned room with smoke. Dmitri said *I love lesbian women*, he said it really sincerely, and then he said *I had an eight month affair with a lesbian, she was really wonderful.* I wondered if a lesbian in a eight month relationship with a man could technically be called a lesbian, but there I was, dripping pink triangles onto the carpet.

It didn't matter that we hadn't gotten rope because Dmitri hadn't thought we were serious about that and didn't want to be tied up anyway. He'd tie us up, though. Oh, sure I thought. As long as we know who's who around here. As long as we know who's wearing the pants. I was getting a little annoyed so I pulled off my boots, leaned back and kissed him. I kissed him and it wasn't so bad as long as I didn't breathe through my nose. He smelled like such a guy. He tasted like a guy too, all thick tongue and Marlboros. I shut my eyes and played with his hair, not so much pretending he was a woman as pretending he wasn't a man. Some sort of benevolent in-between. Liz brought her face over and we all three started kissing together which seemed really cliché and silly but they appeared to like it so I went with it. There were hands moving in various directions and clothes being discarded and Liz was right, Dmitri's dick was huge. It was the weirdest thing I'd ever seen, like a big rhino tusk with a wrinkly turtleneck foreskin. Dmitri was rolling a condom onto it and I was thinking that thing is going to hurt but surprisingly it was only mildly uncomfortable, like going to the gynecologist. Liz was beside us watching and every time our eyes caught I gave her a Meaningful Look. I'm not sure what I was try-ing to communicate, but these looks seemed to be freak-ing her out. I thought maybe it would be better if I kept my eyes closed but I needed to see what was happening so I let them stay open and worked on keeping a calm, cheerful and somewhat aroused look on my face. After being with Ian for two years I was fairly good at this, but I was getting increasingly angry at myself for ending up in a situation where I felt like I had to. It all seemed to be taking a very long time and because I am such a nice person I felt this stupid obligation to make sure I was paying equal attention to both Dmitri and Liz. What I really wanted to do was crawl beneath the bed. When it became unbearable I would fake an orgasm because it gave me the opportunity to yell, and after I was done Dmitri would move back over to Liz. Dmitri, it seemed, was not even close to cumming, and it was unspoken knowledge between us all that this would continue until he did. It was making me very panicky. I flashed a few more Meaningful Looks Liz's way, she returned them with scowls. Dmitri was working her body with the focus of a masseuse and I was wrecking her concentration. I didn't know what to do with myself. My hands were pesky as flies, lighting briefly on Liz's shoulders, Dmitri's back. I moved to the edge of the bed and tried to stay out of their way. Liz looked like she was having a good time, but then so did I. I wasn't sure of anything.

Liz never had an orgasm and she never pretended to. She just lay there with a dreamy look on her face until Dmitri pulled himself off her and followed his dick into the bathroom. Liz kept her position on the bed, propped up on a mound of pillows like a kid home sick from school. She was sweating and breathing funny and I pulled myself across the bed to be beside her. Did He Come Yet Or What I whispered. *I don't care* she said, *I'm through. I can't keep this up all night.* Do You Think He Has A Problem Cumming I asked. Liz shrugged. *You were giving me the craziest looks,* she said, *you were freaking me out. Don't ever do that again.* Liz, This Isn't Ever Going To Happen Again. The bathroom door creaked open and out walked Dmitri looking shy but unashamed. He sat down beside us and rubbed Liz's leg affectionately. Everything seemed impossibly worse now that the sex was over. I wanted Dmitri to go away but he had leaned his back against the bed's plastic head-board and draped his long skinny legs across Liz. He looked pretty comfy. I tossed the two of them a smile and hopped off the bed into the bathroom. Dmitri had left the seat up and the window open, the cold linoleum sent goosebumps popping up my body. I sat on the toi-let and shivered. Stress always whacks me in the guts. My stomach was cramped and gurgling like a backed up sewer. I reached towards the sink and flicked on the water, hoping to drown out my small explosions of diar-rhea. I was feeling increasingly miserable and wanted nothing more than to crawl into that second empty bed with its cool pastel sheets free of sex and sweat. Liz would have to understand that I was just too sick to share the burden of entertaining Dmitri. I stood, wiped, flushed the toilet and watched in horror as the brown sludge rose to the top and spilled over. It was more than I could handle right then and I began to cry, backing away from the creeping tide until I bumped up against the sink. There was nothing I could do to stop it. I leaned over and slapped the lid down but it poured out from beneath, drooling fat puddles onto the linoleum. And my body still wasn't finished with me. I had forced it to endure an episode of dick and it was going to make me pay. I hung my head over the sink and puked. It was as if my body was trying to purge itself of the entire experience. I puked til my heaves brought nothing, then rinsed my mouth with water. Bile had turned my teeth to chalkboard and nails, and the panic in my belly grew as I surveyed what I had done to the bathroom. I decided not to deal with it. The most important thing was to get my rickety body into that bed and let sleep finish me off.

Back in the real world, sex was definitely over. Side by side they sat, Liz with bedcovers pulled up to her chin, Dmitri smoking cigarettes and looking rather pleased with himself. You would hardly believe that soft shriveled thing on his thigh was the very same penis that made me suck in my breath with dread. It looked harmless as a newborn mouse spent from suckling, pink and damp and furless. I made as little eye contact as possible and threw myself into the empty bed. I'm Really Sick I said, digging my way under the blankets. They murmured at me in alarmed voices, but their concern was less about my health than about having to deal with each other one on one. Liz was going to be furious with me for leaving her alone in this weird scenario, but since it was her big idea to begin with I didn't feel much guilt. I figured that Dmitri would soon leave and we would both have the luxury of big beds all to ourselves, to sleep off the evening like a bad drunk. But Dmitri never left. He lay in that bed with Liz all night, rolled on his side and looking right at me. Whenever I peeked out from beneath the covers I found his big eyes open and searching for connection. I'd give him the same polite smile I'd been smiling all night and roll over, wishing I had Liz to press myself against. It was creepy. He had this dreamy look on his face. My panic-sick stomach kept me tossing all night, and each time I laid in his direction I would sneak a look at him, unable to believe he was still awake and staring. He moved his mouth at me. What? I whispered. *You were wonderful,* he whispered. I thought about how under different circumstances I might have met Dmitri

117

and thought he was an OK guy, but now I would certainly hate him forever. He left as the morning sun came seeping through the blinds, and only then was I able to sleep. Liz shook me awake sometime later. As I had guessed, she was pissed at me for abandoning her, but she was more pissed at Dmitri for staying all night. *What was he thinking*, she fumed, *we're all boyfriend-girlfriend now?* I didn't want to talk about it. I'm Really Sick, I said, but Liz had little sympathy. She once had to have emergency surgery because the little thingies that hang off your fallopian tubes got all twisted together in her belly, and she felt no one could ever feel pain like the pain she felt then. *I don't want to hear it*, she said, *you don't know what sick is.* Liz really could be a bitch sometimes. Still, she climbed into bed with me and we watched TV until the maid came banging at the door.

When I told Liz that I might — how did I say it, Try My Hand At The World's Oldest Profession, making it sound light, even campy, a Broadway musical with a chorus of wholesome big-hearted prostitutes — Liz immediately brought up our night with Dmitri. *Yeah Michelle* she laughed this laugh that was more like a snort, and rolled her eyes to Teri. *You can't go near a guy without puking and shitting all over yourself.* Teri giggled. I understood that I was somewhat of a juvenile in the eyes of Liz and Teri. Michelle the bouncy little dyke, safely playing in a bubble of sugar and spice and everything nice, wholly lacking the tough inner machinery needed to descend into the world of men. But I had only just been there. Liz knew little about my years spent catering to the oversexed Ian; I doubted that even during her time as Promiscuous Party Girl did she ever have to endure as many episodes of heterosexual sex as I did with my boyfriend. It made me nuts to be so misunderstood, cast as naive, virginal in the stupidest sense, weaker than them. Whenever I considered prostitution — and the instances increased as I watched Liz and Teri taking off for another day of play while I schlepped to my practically minimum wage food service job — all I could think about was my time with Ian. I knew that it was possible to endure really horribly bad sex and live. It did not need to damage you. Maybe the worst part of the sex I had with Ian was wondering why I hated it so much, this thing I was supposed to love, but that mystery was gone now. Or maybe the worst was how Ian loved me, right, and he never, never knew how much I loathed everything we did with our bodies — that I could so thoroughly fool this person who supposedly knew me so well, that he never detected the falseness of my orgasms, how I quietly manipulated everything to have it end quickly with minimal work — isn't that what whores do? But there would be no sense of betrayal with a stranger. There'd be cash. And limitless free time, oceans of it. Of course I could have shitty sex with men. Duh. Sign Me Up, I said to Liz, and when she realized I was serious you could see little dollar signs pop up in her eyes like an old fashioned cash register. With the both of us making money like that we'd be rich. The woman who ran the agency didn't even ask to meet us first, she had so much faith in Liz and Teri. *You two are classy* she'd said to them numerous times. I guess most of the workforce were more traditionally slutty in appearance, didn't have the high-class call-girl air about them that Liz and Teri exuded. Liz and Teri were Escorts.

My first call was with an old, droopy guy named Martin who lived in Back Bay, right off Newbury Street, blocks away from Copley where a new generation of kids sat hugging their illegal bottles and ollieing off the library stairs. I was at Liz and Teri's waiting for the cab to come and bring me into my new profession. I was shoveling cold spoonfuls of Ben & Jerry's into my mouth and washing it down with tequila from the big bottle Liz kept stashed on top of the fridge. I had Liz's clothes on my body, the beginning of a certain ritual. My own would never do. I wore her makeup, from a dusty bag in the medicine cabinet, and my neck was damp with one of her awful perfumes. I did not look like myself and that made sense. Liz and Teri had already gone on their own calls that night so I was alone when the taxi honked and drove me to this ornate, old-fashioned Bostonian brownstone. Did the cab driver know I was a whore. I realized that it was probably a regular part of a cab driver's job to shuttle whores to and from their tricks. Something I'd never thought about. Martin's apartment was spacious, slightly messy, decorated with plants that grew tall as trees towards the high ceilings. *Would you like some wine?* he asked. I would like to get it over with. Liz had told me to expect this, a pretense of civility, small talk, as if what was happening was actually a blind date arranged by benevolent friends. I drank the wine, white, a big goblet of it. Martin was pathetic. I had expected as much. He was flabby in a way that seemed gross against the backdrop of his opulent apartment. He was blabbing about his work, the big names he worked with who of course I had never heard of and he clucked and said *oh you really should know who so-and-so is* like I had some cultural deficit. I am just so sure we fit each other's expectations perfectly. The bedroom was dim with lots of arty, obvious statues of naked men and naked women and he casually dropped the artists' names and of course I did not know them and they were stupid besides. On a rocking chair that faced the bed was a stuffed animal, a teddy bear named Fatso, and as Martin took my hand and wrapped it around his nasty little dick he said *Oh that's Fatso, I hope you're not shy, Fatso likes to watch.* I had not yet been thrust into the weirdo world of human sexuality, so I did not think that Martin had himself a little teddy bear fetish, no, I thought that there was a hidden camera peering out at us from Fatso's fluffy innards. It was all I could think about, this pervy old freak videotaping me, the idea of the moment not ending when I left but having its own life, re-experienced endlessly by Martin and his friends, if he had any. Well who cares fuck it. It'll be my Certain Sacrifice, to be released on the eve of my fame. *Fatso's watching you* Martin cooed. I couldn't believe I was having sex with this man. It was like a movie. Thinking of it like that made it kind of funny, and the more I thought about it the funnier it really was until it was hilarious, that a girl could sink to this, the ultimate depths of femininity right, the worst case scenario of womanhood, and that it meant absolutely nothing, this was funny. And strangely liberating, not in a I've-Reclaimed-My-Sexuality way because there was nothing of mine to be claimed here. It was the feeling of another societal myth shattering in my cunt, hitting bottom only to discover there was no bottom, only me, and it was possible to go to these places and come back unscathed like a Persephone eating not a few seeds but the whole bleeding pomegranate and flipping off Hades as she skipped out of Hell. It was weird to be on Newbury Street afterwards, a hundred dollars in my pocketbook and a gross KY dampness in my underwear. I needed to hail a cab. I needed to hail a cab without bumping into any acquaintances who were surely out there, cruising this artsy neighborhood on a balmy Friday night, wondering why I was dressed like a goddamn fool. I had a new stink on me, part guy, part latex, part fabricated female. I washed it all off in Liz's shower, pulled on my favorite black catsuit and we walked together to a blues bar in her neighborhood. *How was it* she wanted to know, *are you ok?* It was like asking someone if they feel older on their birthday. I'm Fine, I laughed, I'm Totally Fine. I told her about Fatso the bear who liked to watch, and for weeks we crank called Martin, singing into his phone *There was a bear who liked to watch and Fatso was his name-o! F-A-T-S-O, F-A-T-S-O, F-A-T-S-O and Fatso was his name-o!* Later I worked at an in-call. A bunch of women worked there. Teri would bring the most exotic foods to the place — wasabi chips that made your nose burn and get runny, miniature french pickles, fuchsia bowls of borscht with an island of sour cream floating on top. If Teri was there the tv would be on and she'd be on the couch, long legs tucked beneath her, a book on her lap. One time Tristan, one of the few of her and Liz's friends that knew, called in a flurry of excitement. *Put on channel nine* he said *they're busting whores on COPS.* It was nighttime which was always particularly creepy, just me and Teri and the screen lit up with big tough men interrogating crying women. One in particular was the weak link, skinny white woman, stringy blonde hair clinging in clumps to her wet face. The cops knew she had a son, that's what they were doing to her. *Would you like for your son to know his mommy's a prostitute.* That was the language they used, *Mommy*, and I watched the woman shrink beneath their words and thought about how the less shame you have the less weapons people have against you. The woman was nodding, crying, *I know, I'm disgusting, I'm a terrible mother.* Oh Teri I Can't Watch This, but we had to. It was an education, like when the woman from the rape crisis center spoke at my women's studies class at Salem State, saying *never take a shower, as much as you will want to,* preparing us for something awful. This is how cops play. Who they really wanted was the madam, and they used this scared woman to get her, a squad of blue jumping out of the dark as she walked to her car. Oh Teri, Turn It Off. *That's what I would do*, she said. *I wouldn't go to jail, I'd talk.* Well I Wouldn't. I'd Call The ACLU And Turn It Into A Media Circus For The Decriminalization Of Prostitution, Be A Hero.

Every now and then there would be Jacquie who was really Cindy Lou, the way Teri was Rachel and I was Allison. Cindy Lou was a big blonde, working-class, beautiful. She came from Lynn Lynn City Of Sin and had that awful just-outside-Boston accent I love. She had a day job selling stamps at the post office, she'd strut into the apartment sometime after 5 o'clock wearing her striped work shirt with the little blue eagle. Me and Cindy Lou had the same birthday. She'd have a fruity pink bottle of wine in her bag, we'd bring the cordless phone up onto the roof and drink, all of Boston falling beneath us.

Cindy Lou had this crazy dildo she'd bring to work, it was that translucent pink plastic little girls' jellyfish sandals are made of and it was filled with different colored marbles that rolled around when you turned it on, writhing like a thing alive. Fascinating and kind of gross. Cindy Lou was a witch. On slow days she burned pubic hair in the sink and made the whole place stink. She brought in this thick red penis candle and carved our address into it with a steak knife, set it burning on top of the television. Cindy Lou was older and had been working longer, she'd survived the Magic Johnson Famine that had whores across the country waiting sadly by their silent phones while the terrified tricks thought about AIDS for possibly the first time in their lives. Slow nights made her anxious.

Tess really enjoyed her work so naturally we all hated her. She'd totter into the living room on these unbelievable gold-tipped heels and collapse on the couch with a moan. *Was he good! I shoulda been paying him!* Tess talked with a lisp that made her comments even harder to listen to. It is telling that I can't remember her real name. Tess was her whore name, but she really became it. She was older than all of us and had been working forever. She had been part of the big Boston mafia sex & drugs ring that got busted in the 70s and made headlines in all the papers. She lived out on Cape Cod with her disabled fisherman husband and all their kids, she supported the whole bunch of them and this did elicit some compassion. I mean, can you imagine. There were many instances of tricks trying to get you to do something out of the question by saying *well I saw Tess last week and she did.* We couldn't figure out who was lying.

It was kind of bad whore etiquette to do the unsafe or unusual because then the men would expect it from everyone. There was Joanie who deserves her own story, and Anna who was young and not there long. She was confused by my lesbianism. *Well, do you enjoy it,* she asked, meaning work. No! I said, horrified. Do You? I was worried about Anna. She also worked for an out-call agency, and she quit the house when she realized the same men who saw her through the agency also came to see us at the apartment. She thought they only saw her. She thought they were her boyfriends.

There was Lyn the owner, she ran the whole operation. She also took calls, something many madams don't do, so that endeared her to us, but we were giving her a cut of our money so it was impossible for a boss dynamic not to develop. Lyn was always firing me, for not wearing makeup or shaving my body. I would have to calm her down. Lyn, If You Want Me To Shave Just Ask, It's No Problem. *I did ask you!* And I Shaved. *But it's all grown back she yelled,* exasperated. *You have to shave,* she insisted. *You're costing the house money.* It's true. I would come to the door in this sleeveless black dress with wiry bits of hair creeping out from my armpits and the man would just turn right around and walk back into the elevator. So I kept my pits bare and hid my hairy legs with thick black stockings. Teri, who was also hairy, was furious. *If we have to shave then she should have to go on a diet,* she fumed. *Either we're adhering to the beauty standard or we're not.* Lyn was all rolling tits and hips. Teri called her Venus of Willendorf.

Lyn was always shutting the whole place down. She was paranoid about being busted, and after seeing that cop show I couldn't really blame her. She's the one who'd get it. Lyn was a business major at Boston University, it was hard to believe she was younger than me, she just had so much money. She paid off select cops and kept an expensive lawyer, dropped an envelope now and then to the building manager. But she truly was paranoid. The most inconsequential interaction with a cop would set her off, a speeding ticket would shut us down for two weeks, sending all the whores flipping through the back pages of the Boston Phoenix seeing which agencies were hiring, which agency did you not rip off and maybe could go back to work for. It served to keep you in a strange panicky limbo, making an absurd amount one week and knowing you could be out of a job the next.

I was living at the in-call that winter, working so much there was no point to leave. It was scary. Nowhere to sleep but the beds you took calls on all day. I'd have to do things to make it seem different, sleep with my head at the end of the bed, keep clean sheets and pillows stashed in a closet. The place stunk like sweet chemical cherry from the electric air fresheners, Plug-Ins, Lyn had one jammed into every outlet in the house. She was trying to mask the smell of men but it didn't work, it just made you sick, the combination of men and cherry and latex. I had nightmares a lot, men breaking in. It seemed possible. It was their house, really. This is a hard story to tell, everything being tangled up in every other thing. What was I doing that winter. I was having panic attacks, that is one thing I was doing a lot. And I wasn't eating dairy because it was so unfair to the cows and I was feeling sick from that, waking weak and shaking in the morning, my head light and spinny. I mean, even when I'm on cheese I don't eat correctly, in terms of volume. So I had really narrowed my options and what was I eating, oranges, carrots, I remember waiting for a call and eating a raw yellow pepper. I became obsessed with fat: was I getting enough fat, what if I wasn't, what would happen. I had these jeans that were so big on me, I kept them belted with one of those awful colorful hippie belts, having given up my leather belt in solidarity with the cows. I lived in those jeans and I know they made me look just completely anorexic, like a junkie. One morning I woke up feeling particularly strange and sick, stumbled out into the living room arranged with rented furniture like a movie set, picked up the cordless phone and dialed 1-800-ASK-A-NURSE, I'm sure I was very deep in the clutches of a panic attack. I asked the telenurse what happened if you didn't eat enough fat. She wasn't sure. That 1-800-ASK-A-NURSE is just a front for the pharmaceutical companies, all they know to tell you is what drug you should take. The telenurse flipped through a book and told me that without enough fat you get confused. I was confused. I didn't know what the fuck I was doing. I was making so much money, I had this thick roll of hundred dollar bills that terrified me. I didn't know what to do with it. I was afraid to leave it at the apartment, so whenever I went out I brought it with me, lying in the pocket of my enormous jeans. And I was so weak with hunger, any ambitious thug could have rolled me easy and scored big. I did not know what to do with so much money. My family was poor, I felt guilty buying anything, felt guilty just having it when my mother busted her ass as a nurse, caring for old people who never got better, they just got sicker and sicker until they died. And my little sister who couldn't pay her phone bill or her electric bill or security deposit, whatever it was I paid it, bought her schoolbooks, gave her money to visit New York. Because the money came so quickly it was easy to feel like you hadn't earned it. I would go out drinking and wouldn't let anyone pay for anything, it just didn't seem fair. My friends seemed uneasy but they let me, they were broke. They were a little bit worried about me, but being cosmopolitan urban dykes had the theoretical understanding that not all sex workers are victims and I was in control and all work was prostitution anyway. Thinking I encouraged because who wants to be viewed as a victim, and, at least at the beginning, I believed it. Back when it was this surreal thing I had started doing, why, because my girlfriend was, our friends were and then suddenly I had to move out of my parents' house and tell me, how does a person support themselves. I was such a child right then, I understood nothing, how people paid bills, rent, bought food, how did they afford it. Whoring was the first and only way I had ever supported myself. And there was no grey area, you really felt that. You were either completely OK so no one would worry about you or it was just the worst thing so, OK well quit then. No one's making you do it. It's true. And I couldn't do anything, I mean, I couldn't even think about the whole world stretched out there forever and me alone in the center of it, having to take care of myself. It got to be that bad calls were good because I got to freak out a little and it was justified. The old guy that came in drunk, he was like my grandfather, a big sturdy old guy like that, irish, putting out his cigarettes on his dinner plate. Probably a retired cop. He had this video camera and if you looked through the lens you could watch the video inside. It was a woman drying off from her shower, oblivious, wiping the wet from her body with a towel, framed by her window. He had filmed her. What do you do. Throw the camera on the bed. I Don't Want To Watch That. What do you do. This is your job. You can take little revenges as they present themselves but there are no sex worker superheros. You are paid to be compliant. Don't like it, quit. Does anyone like it. Does anyone quit. I quit. But not then. I went out into the living room, I was freaking out, I told them what happened, the women who were there. This man who had filmed a woman drying off her body. She was just taking a shower, she didn't know she was on stage. *Oh Michelle* said Teri. She meant it. She knew what my stepfather had done, little sneak, poking holes in the walls, bedroom and bathroom. *Oh Michelle* she said, and what else could she say. Don't like it, quit.

That winter our friend Lara became a whore. Big owl glasses over eyes lidded lavender and blue like eggs in spring. Lipstick clinging to the edge of her teeth, big square teeth with a space in the middle. Like me, Lara had no whore clothes, only a need for some money and fast. She and Kate — who my friendship with kind of withered away into hopeless awkwardness once our small affair ended — were moving to Detroit, to do political work and fight the Klan. Kate moved back to Rhode Island to live with her parents and save money that way, and Lara moved into Teri's new apartment with everyone else. We were all homeless whores that winter, there were five of us sleeping on Teri's floor. Lara taught me how to cook and I taught her how to be a girl, makeup all over the bathroom, giggling and pushing each other out of the mirror. There was a plastic bag in the closet stuffed with communal lingerie, garters, teddies, lace panties. The stockings all had runs in them, you had to twist the nylon so the tear ran down the back of your calf, that way the john wouldn't open the door and think you were shabby. We were back to doing out-calls, after a final burst of paranoia had Lyn shutting down the brothel indefinitely. Also in Teri's closet was a cardboard box full of condoms, lubed and unlubed, left over from our brief stint as AIDS educators, when we circled the blocks of the combat zone after midnight, loaded down with rubbers and needles. After about a month everyone got bored and stopped showing up, leaving us all this free latex plus a hazardous waste container of dirty needles that nobody knew what to do with.

Lara had belted on her garters and was in this Victoria's Secret bra the color of dried blood and to tell you the truth she looked ridiculous. She knew it, too. She was laughing like crazy, getting makeup all over her teeth. Lara's hair stood straight up around her head. She didn't make it that way, it's how it went natural. She was in the bathroom, trying to flatten it down with hairspray and gel. She was in the closet trying to find something to wear, nothing fit. She had on this dress of Teri's, life jacket orange and much too big, it hung past her knees and bagged out at her tits. Thick soled shoes like little tanks on her feet. We were moving around with all this nervous energy, drinking red wine and drooling it into our cleavage. Trying to find stockings that weren't completely shredded. Imagine Laverne & Shirley as prostitutes. Imagine them getting drunker and drunker, packing purses full with condoms and lube. The apartment was empty, Teri and Brad were on dates and Liz had gone off on a brief vacation to Tucson, where it was warm. It was good that she was gone. Everything nice about Liz had frozen up with the weather. Even Teri, her best friend for long, had tried to escape her. Teri moved out of their nice south end apartment into this slightly shabby brick building in Jamaica Plain. Liz hadn't been able to find a new place for herself, and like cats or a couple of small orphans we followed Teri into this new place where we slept on the floor. I would turn to curl up onto Liz and she would pull away. *Don't touch me.* What's The Matter? Why Can't I Touch You? *Will you let me sleep!* An attempted kiss in the kitchen — *Cut it out.* Are You Mad At Me? *God, you are so fucking insecure! I'm just trying to cook dinner!* She would go out with her friends, straight people from when she used to be, and I couldn't come. *Don't you have any of your own friends?* I used to. Where had they gone. There was Lara, and she was there and Liz was not and the house felt festive. Boston was cold, snow everywhere and Teri's building was always low on oil so the heating grates blew out this horrible burning smell. I had gotten Lara a job at Premiere which really was the best agency because Janie who ran it knew it was a joke and would give you the scoop on the tricks. *He's cake* she'd say about the easy ones. *Oh, him you can push around, no problem. This one's into the occult, shit like that, ask him to read your tarot cards and you'll kill a half hour.* Premiere's clientele was mostly regulars, the same thirty or forty guys who'd been calling prostitutes forever. What was really great was that Liz and Teri had both worked for Premiere too, so when you got a call odds were someone in the house had already seen him and you could get the full low-down. But Lara's first call was a new guy out in Cambridge. I couldn't tell her anything. Lara was so nervous, she was fumbling with this big wool coat of Teri's and then the cab came and took her away. The agency had a set-up with a cab company in Boston, three or four drivers who knew what was up and would be quiet and polite at first, then loosen up and start asking you all these questions about whoring. It was like being on a talkshow, to feel like such an expert on something. You were from this other world, sitting there in the back seat of the cab. An ambassador of sorts. The drivers were mostly men, carefully sleazy, but one was a woman named Wendy. Wendy was considering joining the agency but was afraid she'd come to think of the tricks as boyfriends. Wendy was a little fucked up. Each time I rode with her she would need to discuss this incident in which her roommate was raped by a friend who crawled in through the window and surely her friend could have fought him off or something, what did I think? It wasn't til after I'd stopped working that I realized it had probably happened to her.

Lara's first trick was a closet case who fell in love with her. She did look like a boy, so tall and no chest. He had her put on this white men's shirt, button-down with a crisp collar, like businessmen wear. He had her keep her clunky shoes on. He fucked her from behind with his hands on her ass and it was no big deal. That was the scariest thing, when you first started whoring. How it seemed like this big thing but really it wasn't and you were fine. You could give yourself a nervous breakdown wondering why you weren't having a nervous break-down. Lara kept asking her trick about the shirt, why he wanted her to wear it, and he would say *don't talk about it* and change the subject. He was a young guy, rich and artsy. He was friends with Ethan Kanin, that writer. He gave Lara a copy of *Emperor of the Air*, she tried to read it but eventually threw it across the room. Another trick was psychic, he told Lara she was a lesbian and had a lover in Rhode Island. Lara would tell all the tricks she was a dyke even though I begged her not to. They'd want to hear all about it. D*o you like big tits, do you do 69?* Do any dykes do 69? It's a magazine thing. I'd see a guy after Lara did and he'd look at my short hair and go *Are you a lesbian too*, wanting to hear a story, make it all seem as gross as himself. I'd say No I Like Men and tell him about my boyfriend, the marine.

Lara was in Boston all winter. She was there for the big snowstorm that knocked out the power and had us dressing for a party by candlelight. Some big art party in the south end, lots of fancy well-paid straight people, girls in short dresses that came slipping through the ice in John Fluevogs. Me and Lara were the dykes, we drank their beer and made fun of them. One boy with dread-locks thought he was real cool, Lara kept calling him slut til he pushed her. She'd walk by him and go *slut*, real low so only he could hear her. *Why're you saying that* he said finally, and knocked her into the wall. Lara was there for Trisha the bike messenger heroin addict who just came out and wanted to sleep with everyone. I did not want to further complicate things with Liz so I avoided Trisha, but Lara took her home to Teri's floor. Things with Lara and Kate were complicated to the point that something like that wasn't a big deal. That was the night that Liz called from Tucson and was such a bitch on the phone that I had to break up with her. I was so upset, sitting on the floor with Trisha and Lara, crying and smoking Trisha's cigarettes. I drank so much wine I slept with a pot by my head and eventually used it. I could hear Lara and Trisha fucking while I puked and they could hear me puking while they fucked. In the morning they brought me water and aspirin and sat with me under the covers.

When Kate called it was night, Lara was lying on the floor reading a book. I had to pretend it was someone else on the phone, I think I acted like it was my sister. A bunch of kids got shot at the school they used to go to. It was a skinhead boy who everyone knew was dangerous, he got a gun and ran around campus shooting people. Everyone knew he was dangerous but nobody knew what to do. He shot a language teacher who was gay and Lara's friend saw it happen, he ran over to help and he got shot too. He died. His name was Galen, and he was Lara's best friend. *Galen's dead* Kate said, *I'll be in Boston tomorrow.* Lara slept that night but I didn't. I told her in the morning, when Kate called from the bus station needing directions. *Why's Kate here?* A Boy Shot People At Your School, I said. Someone Died, Someone You Know. I remember her face, I never had to tell someone something like that. I remember her face, like my mother when she saw the x-rays of my grandmother's lungs. My mother was a nurse, no one had to tell her anything. Lara said *was it Galen oh my god was it Galen* and I said I Don't Know. I wanted Kate to be there. Lara was crazy, she was crying before she even knew. Then the doorbell rang and it was Kate, Lara crying and yelling all over her, punching her shoulders *what happened was it Galen, Galen's dead?* and Kate said yes and Lara howled. She just howled. She was like an animal, so completely human, just an animal howling. I went into the kitchen and started cleaning, wiping down the table, rinsing wine from glasses. Lara's howls filled the house, I had to move through them to get to the sink. She sobbed til she puked, in the bathroom, the wooden door shut. Teri's new house was old, the walls shook with sobbing, you could feel it beneath your feet like the bass from a loud stereo. It was in all the papers that week, the lead on the six o'clock news. The school knew he was getting bullets in the mail. They knew and they didn't do anything. All Lara's friends were on TV, crying, talking to the cameras. The news made the school sound like a place for freaks, an art school for outcasts who couldn't deal with high school. Like of course something like this would happen. Look at all the students, leather jackets, fucked up hair. Galen's parents were on the news, calm and sad, they said that all Galen's friends were welcome at their house, they could come and sleep there and go to his funeral. We sat in front of Teri's little TV in her bedroom and watched this and cried. Everyone was calling on the phone for Lara, the crying kids from the television, her mother in Ohio, her sister in California with Visualize World Peace on her answering machine. Lara came to Boston and filled the house completely then was gone. She went to the funeral, she went back to the school and all the services and then she went to Detroit, to fight the Klan.

I felt mildly crazy after the breakup but who doesn't. Breaking up meant back to my parents. I was 21 which I guess is too old to still be at home but the thought of rent and bills scared me, I didn't understand how it worked. You couldn't talk to my mother on bill day, she'd be at the table with all these papers and a calculator, chain smoking. You stayed out of the kitchen like she'd just mopped the linoleum. You stayed in the parlor and watched tv or you walked down to the store or something. I was in no hurry to grow up. My parents had moved during my relationship. My mother got the settlement she'd been waiting for since throwing her back out lifting a patient 5 years ago and was able to Get Out Of Chelsea. She bought a house in Malden. Malden was on a slower track to hell than Chelsea, there was a park across the street that she felt safe walking her new dog in. She'd been on my ass for months about packing up my room. I hate domestic things plus I didn't like being reminded that I still lived at home, that Liz's sunny apartment with the smooth wood floors hadn't really been mine. *I'm going to throw it all in boxes* my mother threatened and I said Sure Fine I Don't Care Throw It All In The Trash If You Want. I was really into burning bridges right then. All my memorabilia, my books and decorations, had been collected while I was straight so I felt like they really didn't apply anymore. I wanted to be reborn pure as a lesbian with no past. I came into the world with a short haircut and a Queers Bash Back sticker slapped on my ass. My mom dumped my bedroom into boxes and that's what I was demoted to when I left Liz, this big white room with a sputtering radiator and a stack of boxes containing all the shit my life had accumulated. I was kind of depressed. I discovered that all my friends had moved to New York. I had no one to hang out with. I had no job. I'd been lying to my parents for months, working as a prostitute but telling them I was doing telephone fundraising for a non-profit environmental group, so every night between 5 and 10 I'd have to go somewhere. I'd hop a bus to Boston, sit in a cafe and ponder my situation. As I said, I was mildly crazy so I was wearing lots of makeup. Breakups leave me with this intense compulsion to change my appearance. I had thick dark stuff like bruises around my eyes, lipstick wiped off on napkins before eating. A white turtleneck and the tiniest fuzzy leopard miniskirt, white cotton tights, fancy shoes with impossible heels. I sat around drinking tea and reading the gay newspaper until I figured I should stop pretending and get a job since there was no way I could whore from my parents' house. I mean, I guess I could've, there was a phone in my bedroom to take calls from, and I normally dressed slutty and stayed out late so that wouldn't have been suspicious but Come on. How twisted. My mother smoking cigarettes in front of the television, I kiss her cheek and dash off to a call. That this was even an option made me realize something really strange had happened to my life. Something to do with Liz. I got a job at the non-profit group I'd been pretending to work at. I was on the telephone making people feel bad about pollution so they'd give me money on a credit card. I guess I was still hustling. Liz was back from her vacation in Arizona, I called her at her life where things were going as usual, full of money and free time and men. She couldn't believe I had gotten a job so quickly and I felt pretty proud, like See I Don't Need You. Because I met Liz at such a moment of change in my life, we both thought she created me. She was disappointed that I had gotten on with my life and for the first time with Liz I felt like I had the upper hand. It wouldn't last long. I had left a bunch of my tapes in her car, on the floor. Probably getting all stepped on and cracked. And there was a stack of my best 80s records in Teri's living room and I wanted them back. *You'll have to come get them* she said, so I did. Liz buzzed me into the worn brick apartment that had only just been my home. She talked on the phone the whole time I was there, she was giving me Attitude. She had a face that expressed disgust perfectly. She looked at me like that while I walked around the place collecting my things. *Michelle* she spat into the phone. *She's getting her shit.* Probably she was talking to one of the tribe of ex-boyfriends that were always on the phone or drinking wine at her table or anywhere but far away like they should've been. John the little weasel who liked to argue with me about sexism. Tom the artist who looked like Fabio and was still in love with her. Liz loved to move through the male gaze while pretending she wasn't caged by it. She was constantly talking about which guy was attracted to her, in this outraged voice because we were lesbians therefore outraged by male desire but she just couldn't stop inviting these guys over for dinner parties. Then going on about so-and-so staring at her tits all night over the pasta. Whatever. I felt free beneath the weight of her disgust as I grabbed my Mark Almond albums and headed for the closet to collect the little bits of my self I had stored there. My go-go boots slumped sad in the corner. I was taking them home, wherever that was. Saying goodbye to the cat was hard because I felt like he was mine the way I felt like most of Liz's life was mine. I stood by the door as she talked on the phone. *What* she said. My Tapes Are In Your Car. She sighed heavily and got off the phone. Liz drove a little red car, and because I had given her a chunk of money to pay off her parking tickets I felt like it was my car too. I thought about taking the hubcaps as some kind of trophy. There were tapes scattered all over the floor. Liz had awful taste in music, she really loved Cat Stevens. As a compromise we listened to the same Nirvana and Cure tapes over and over, but whenever we fought she'd pop in Steely Dan to remind me that it was her car and her life and I was only a guest. Well, Bye I said, weighed down with all my shit. *Wait, we should talk.* She had her soft voice on now, the one she used for talking to children or asking for money. Why. *Well... this feels wrong to me. I need to talk to you, please just take a walk with me.* No I said knowing I would but wanting to hold onto this power a little longer. *Really, I've been having a hard time, I need to talk to someone.* We put my stuff in her hallway and began our walk through the grey New England streets. It was February, really cold and I was in a red miniskirt. Because I went to Catholic school for 9 years I thought that your legs were like your face and you didn't have to cover them in the winter. Trudging through the snow in my holy plaid skirt and kneesocks. *This is a hard time of the year for me,* Liz began. She reached out for my hand. *I always get crazy right around the time I was raped. I just freak out and fuck everything up.* My heart plopped into my belly. Oh Liz, I said. Oh Fuck Wow I Didn't Know.... She squeezed my hand. Liz had been raped a couple years ago, she didn't talk about it in detail but I knew that it had happened in the snow, in a snowbank, and Brad who had been her roommate then told me about how she had sat in the shower with all her clothes on and wouldn't talk. Later, while going through her things I found the transcripts from the trial and sat on the floor and cried, reading about how he told her he loved her as he wrapped his fist around her hair and yanked her head to the ice. Later still she told me she lied about the whole thing. But right then on the February sidewalk I wanted to lie down with her and pet her, make her feel safe. I knew I was put on this earth to help women. She was my girlfriend. *Let's go out for dinner* she said, *my treat.*

So I was back in Liz's clutches and I was afraid to quit my job. I started whoring again, because it was there and it paid well and me and Liz had made up and concocted this plan to move to Arizona. Going to Arizona sounded like going to Mars. I imagined rough red rocks and crazy looking plants that hurt too much to touch. Drunk in a bar I looked at Liz's deeply tanned face, the sharp cliffs of her cheekbones, You Look Like Arizona, I told her. *What?* I couldn't explain it. In Tucson Arizona it would be warm all the time and we could live in a little house made of mud. Liz talked about it and it sounded like a lush paradise, lemon and orange trees on the streets, aloe plants in your yard to snip and gut and rub into your skin. We would open an art gallery, we would paint and sculpt and write and be far from our horrible pasts that sprang from the New England landscape like the lifeless winter trees. I knew I would leave, always I had known that. I had imagined New York but who cares. We would head west at the end of the winter. Until then, I would hold onto my fundraising shifts at the nonprofit. I just knew that it could happen again with Liz, her incredible meanness even though right then she was a docile rape survivor, quiet and vulnerable in my arms. She could strike again and I would need a job. So I called guilty liberals from 5 to 10, took the train to Liz's, hopped into whore clothes and went on a call. Once I had an afternoon call at the Howard Johnson's near Fenway, a lawyer who defended women in sexual harassment cases. *It's a shame what men get away with* he said and I jerked him off with hand lotion. I took the train straight to my other job and bumped into these Queer Nation boys me and Liz would crank call when we were bored. They knew it was us and they kept threatening to call the cops. *How revolutionary* Liz would tease them and hang up. They really had me, there on the subway in pumps and full makeup, like blush and pink lipstick, all of it. My purse full of condoms and lube. I just looked at my feet and let them have their moment of triumph. At my legitimate job everyone said I looked so pretty. It always made me barf, how people I knew would be as impressed by my costume as the dumb, salivating tricks. I thought I looked boring and normal like a girl I'd never want to talk to. Thanks, I said, I went out to lunch with my girlfriend's parents, Legal Seafood. My co-workers were handling my exquisite beaded purse and I was terrified at it spilling open, condoms and cash falling onto my calling station. Eventually this double life became too stressful so I quit my noble & respectable job at the non-profit and went back to the agency full time.

Liz was going through money like water, she always had. It was that wealthy Connecticut upbringing, her family was so old money it was practically genetic. If I let her out of my sight for a minute she'd show up with 200 dollar shoes or some evening gown she'd never have the occasion to wear and I'd have to be the heavy. Liz We're SAVING. For TUCSON. And we'd fight. *Don't tell me what to do. Don't tell me what to spend my money on. You can go buy yourself a dress too you know, I don't care.* But then we'd have nothing at all, so I hoarded my money and took us to Tucson, the trunk packed tight with all of Liz's pretty clothes.

Patricide and Prostitution
Tucson 1992

This was my life in Tucson. Early Tucson, before I was whoring, when I wasn't even working at all. What bliss. It seemed natural, Tucson so slow and lazy. Did anyone work? Not me. I was up with the sun in the toxic gold of my bedroom. It took 12 cans of spray paint to make the walls glow like that, my trigger finger cramped and sticky and I blew my nose gold for a week. Climb out of bed and yank down the black flannel curtains so the day could begin. Make some food in the little yellow kitchen, tea with honey, avocado on pita, bring it all into the backyard and eat naked on a towel in the sun. Whoever lived in the adobe before we did forgot to cancel their newspaper so I had that each morning, spread out on the dead needles that dripped off the Palo Verde tree, learning which Arizona politicians I was supposed to hate and which were good or at least hopeful. The backyard was marvelous. Small but fenced so you could get naked though I kept my panties on because I was afraid of that Arizona sun on my pussy. The Palo Verde tree hung over a rickety shed that certainly housed scorpions, and its needles would drop into piles on the roof, little nests for the cat to curl up and sleep in. The cat was slinky and quick, he'd bring Liz fear-frozen lizards, drop them by her head as she laid naked beside me. Oh Pal, I cooed, Don't You Love Me? Where Are My Lizards? The next night I found a caterpillar on my pillow, torn and leaking yellow. There were cactuses in the backyard, that happens in Tucson. They seemed alive to me in ways that other plants didn't, extra-terrestrial. A fat spiny pod with a crown of yellow blossoms. Another was so big it looked ancient, like a dinosaur plant. Someone told me it's where tequila comes from. The leaves, if that's what they were, curled into spears at the tip. I had cuts on my leg from walking too close. The desert was a ruthless place. All the animals were poison and even the plants had these weapons. There was a broken wooden swing hanging from the Palo Verde tree, rickety but you could sit in it if you were tiny like me. Hippies used to live there, we found chunks of their pottery jutting out of the dirt like ancient artifacts. I know I'm making this all sound so nice, but you have to know that the whole time I was in Tucson I was losing my mind. I was gone. Because of incest and male abuse. I had had some incest, though it wasn't the physical kind. It was holes cut into walls for my stepfather to attach his eyes to. I was a peepshow. Tucson was the aftermath. The horror of knowing someone and living with them and even thinking you're lucky and then wham and now you know that every person is really two people and how can you ever know what the other half is up to. At least with Liz it was obvious, mean and controlling most of the time but there was a nice Liz too and occasionally you caught a glimpse. Sometimes at bedtime, when she curled herself on top of me and was sweet. I could fall asleep like that and wake up with hope, and however the day destroyed it, it could be back in my arms at bedtime.

We went to Mexico when my sister Leicia came to visit. We'd been talking about it for a while — Liz wanted mexican blankets, brightly striped and they would look beautiful in our golden bedroom, and I wanted to go to another country. I couldn't believe I was living so close to one, but then Tucson seemed entirely like another planet, with alien shrubbery and vicious little creatures. When I thought of Mexico I thought of fierce, angry color; Frieda Kahlo's thick heart; chalky skeletons posed at an altar. The virgin of Guadeloupe draped in a robe of stars and shooting swords of light from her head. My sister's visit was a nightmare. She really should have spent her spring break in Miami or Daytona rather than vacationing at my nervous breakdown. Me and my mean girlfriend in a squat adobe, plotting the overthrow of the patriarchy and hating everyone. Of course Liz hated my sister and her long, polished hair, her bag of fruity toiletries. On her very first night in Tucson I sat Leicia down on the couch and told her that me and Liz were prostitutes. I figured why waste time. Why wait til the pager was sounding its shrill beep and Liz was tumbling through the house in a blonde wig and heels. I wasn't even a prostitute right then, the agreement having been that I would work my ass off in Boston, earning the money for our departure, and once in the desert it was Liz's turn to support us. I had stayed in touch with Lyn from the in-call back in Boston, because she was a good job reference. She was actually incorporated, whatever that means, so she could pretend to be a legitimate business and I could pretend to have been, what, a receptionist, office manager, human resources. She kept calling us on the telephone: she's getting out of the business — no, she's going to buy a condo and open a real high-class place. She's going to go on the circuit, this mythical network run by who knows, they take the cream of the crop and fly them to other cities to work for a week, two weeks, a month. You make an extraordinary amount of money because they cater to very wealthy men who will pay extra for the luxury of never bumping into you on the street or in a restaurant. To be assured that you only exist in that moment, for them. The circuit wouldn't take Lyn, she weighed too much. She got lipo-suction, they still wouldn't take her. Teri worked there for a little while after Liz and I left, she said it was crazy. Lyn hired these girls, they were in high school, they came to the apartment after classes. Of course she got busted. She got out of it somehow, paid off the appropriate peo-ple, set herself back up and then what happened. A cop raped a whore, a woman on the street who was crafty and kept the condom he'd used, plump with his come, she delivered it to the hospital and the guy was caught, no way out. It was a real war, cops busting whores all over Boston, the streets, the agencies, the houses, Lyn. She kept calling us out in the desert. She wanted to set something up in Tucson, stay with us while she got her shit together. We even got a letter, desperate. We never called her back. Despite my unemployment there in Tuc-son I still felt like a prostitute. I was existing right then courtesy of prostitution, and anyway, once you crossed that line I figured you were branded for life. I mean, the concept, the whole notion of being a whore, doesn't it have to do with some inherent ability or capability, like if I was fucking a guy for cash last month but now was unemployed, was I still a prostitute? I felt like I was still a prostitute. I told my sister I was a prostitute and she heard it with the brave blankness of someone who has

146

heard too much in one year to be fazed by anything. Really she should have gone to New York or Montreal. The desolate flatness of Tucson terrified her. *What do you DO here?* she asked. What did I do. I made stir fry and drank wine and watched the sun set in the desert. Tiptoed around my psychopathic girlfriend, planned the revolution. Liz really hated my sister's presence in our house. She knew that having a sane outside observer around would disrupt the comfortable flow of our dysfunctional relationship. I was torn and anxious. The showdown between my sister and Liz, or me and Liz, or me and my sister or whatever interpersonal disaster that was doomed to occur, began to form like mold on an old cup of coffee the minute Leicia dropped her bags on our floor. It was an awful week. Leicia wouldn't get in the car because Liz had been hitting the bong all morning. *She's stoned* my sister hissed at me in the hallway. She's Always Stoned, I hissed back. I'd Be More Afraid To Drive With Her Sober. Liz wouldn't take Leicia to KFC, because of the chickens. She Just Wants Mashed Potatoes, I pleaded. My sister lived on mashed potatoes. Liz was offended by Leicia's bathing suit, a nuclear orange bikini with more padding and wires than a medical brace. *I don't think Liz treats you good*, Leicia whispered. It was the horrible morning I almost amputated Liz's finger. She was trying to teach me how to drive, way out in the desert, where I wouldn't kill anything. Actually it was out even past the desert, where the noble green cactuses had been knocked down for cattle ranching. Just flat dead ground for miles and miles. Liz was teaching me to do a three-point-turn and I backed the car up into a sign. It was really small, neither of us had seen it, a thin yellow rectangle that had wedged itself into the metal of the door. Liz hopped out of the car, pried it off with her fingers. *Drive*, she said, and I pressed down on the gas but the car was in reverse. The sign cut deep into her skin and she screamed at me *put it in forward!* I was of course hysterical. I just knew if I drove a car that someone would get hurt. All the red color had drained from Liz's face and was leaking out through her finger. She was going to kill me. We were so far from town and she had to drive us back there, gripping the wheel with her numb and bleeding hand. *I can't feel anything* she said. You could see a ghost of bone beneath all the dripping red. What if I ruined her finger? What if she couldn't ever use it again? She'd break up with me, she icily informed me. I Didn't Do It On Purpose! I was crying and she was telling me to shut up. She had no patience. She wasn't crying. Two coyotes crossed the road and we almost ran them over. They were tan like the dry ground, they looked just like dogs, with soft bits of tongue slipping out of their mouths. Back at the house everything was crazy. Brad, who had come from Boston to stay with us inspected the hurt finger and my sister hovered in the doorway like a scared little kid. *Get away from me* Liz said. I was still crying. *She shouldn't be so mean* my sister said. *You didn't mean it.* I Can't Believe You Said You'd Break Up With Me I said later, when we knew her hand would live. I finally stopped crying but had those annoying hiccups like a blubbering toddler. *How could I look at all your good fingers and not hate you* she said simply. Then, *Can you please get away from me?* Where was I supposed to go? Tuck myself into a little corner of the adobe like my sister? Leicia had eventually just left

148

the house, before Liz's volatile wrath turned on her again. Liz — *Can you just leave me alone?* I pushed through the screen door, hearing it fly back on its busted hinges with a metallic slap. Our neighborhood was blocks and blocks of these sweet southwestern houses, dangerous tangles of cactus in the front yards, wind-chimes and strings of wrinkled chilies hanging from porches. The stink of orange blossoms sweet enough to gag you, hanging from trees right there on the street. In a few more months you'd be able to reach up and grab yourself a piece of fruit, just like that. I bought myself a pack of Marlboro Lights and a little notebook at the Circle K. Lots of punks hung out in the parking lot there, boys with bright mohawks. They sat on top of the pay phones, smoking. Me and Liz would drive by them in the car, both of us in our shapeless indian hippie dresses, listening to the Beatles and Liz would look at the punks and go *Hi, Why don't you try doing something new?* Through our neighborhood ran a ravine, maybe a river once, maybe never. It cut through people's yards and through tunnels hollowed beneath the street. I took my Circle K purchases down to where it passed behind a frat house, where the street was painted with greek symbols. I climbed down from the sidewalk, a slight slope, down to where trees grew and shaded the ditch littered with beer bottles and general trash, tons of cigarette butts which I added to generously. I had quit smoking so long ago, and it seemed like a great time to start again. I found a piece of concrete, a chunk of sidewalk wrenched from the street and dumped there, I smoked and I cried and I wrote about escape. I needed a place to go, a place other than Boston, a place where I could have a life that was new. There were hummingbirds buzzing around the ravine, they hovered like spaceships and took off fast. Deadly looking dragonflies and their iridescent wings. I wrote about how much the trees must hate living there in that trashy dried-up creekbed. I apologized to them. Maybe if I stayed in Tucson I would make it my mission to clean up our neighborhood ravine. So much was happening right then, in the world outside of Tucson. There was a massive march on Washington, queers from all over the country were going there to yell and march and fight the fight that Liz and I were supposed to be fighting, though all we ever really fought was each other. I could go to D.C., I could meet girls who were nice. I knew there were nice girls somewhere because I knew that I was nice and I knew there were no anomalies in nature. I remember hearing about a punk rock house there at the capital, the people who lived there were punk and political, maybe they would take me in and let me join their revolution. By the time I was halfway through my pack of cigarettes I had written a plan involving Greyhound and the pile of money that was meant to set me and Liz up in the desert. But I didn't go. Liz read my notebook. She said that I had to have wanted her to or else I wouldn't have just left it there on the futon. She flipped when she saw my escape plan. It was later that day, the day of the nearly chopped-off finger. *God, I was upset, I almost lost my finger! I'm sorry I yelled at you I love you Please don't leave We just got started here It's going to be better I just got scared I know I can't treat you like that.* Liz followed me through the house, into the bathroom where I climbed beneath the roar of the shower but still could hear her.

She pulled back the wet plastic curtain. *I am so sorry.* My sister peeked her head in timidly. *Are we still going to Mexico?* she asked. So we went to Mexico, with my sister and with Brad. Nogales, a border town. On one side was Burger King, then a tall fence crowned with swirls of razor, then another country. We pushed through a revolving door, like entering a mall. That easy.

How could I not feel like an asshole in Mexico. I've lived my whole life in predominantly latino cities and all I know of spanish is puta. And agua, from Sesame Street. Back in America I was a considerably oppressed lesbian feminist revolutionary, but that got parked in the lot with the car. We were shopping. For mexican blankets, and those skeleton figures I loved. We moved through the loud streets and I recognized the faces of the men who worked the small shops hung with bright blankets and leather wallets and cheap cheap liquor. They were the same faces I showed to my tricks: blameful, superior and wanting their money. I bought things, a sun and a moon, incredibly blue, dark and bright. Mexico was a riot of people and noise, and all the colors I'd expected. Sad donkeys in party hats stood on corners, a trot away from death. You could get your picture taken with them. We ate in a small, empty restaurant. Leicia apologized to Liz for the steak she was eating. Liz shrugged. Leicia kept wanting to take pictures and me and Liz were mortified. We wanted to be down with the locals, travelers not tourists, but really. Give me a break. The men all thought Brad was our communal boyfriend. *Oh, you have two ladies* one guy said, and Brad snapped back *they have one, I have none. Buy your lady some earrings* urged a man at a jewelry shop. *She's mad at you, give her ear-*

rings, she's not mad anymore. I didn't think I had any right to be annoyed. I hated being an american. I felt like The Man. I wanted to go back to Tucson where I was marginalized and righteous. Leicia bought a clay Mayan warrior to hang on her wall and Liz bought a stone pipe. We looked in some pharmacies for the xanax we heard you could buy over the counter in Mexico, but no one knew what we were talking about. I had done xanax once and really loved it. We all bought strawberry popsicles and waited in line to leave Mexico. It is of course harder to go out than come in. A plump little girl tried to sell us small boxes of gum and Liz gave her her popsicle. We harassed the border guard, *nice racist job* Liz sneered as we exited into America. I Don't Ever Want To Go To Mexico Again I said. I felt like such an asshole. On the way back to Tucson we stopped at this place, a church like an enormous antique, built by Spanish colonizers a long time ago. It was on a reservation, tired-looking native people directed traffic in the parking lot, sold fried bread and beans under tattered lean-tos. The church was gorgeous. It was intense, big crumbling altars of torn and dying christs, grieving madonnas. It was under renovation or something, tiers of scaffolding lined the walls, framing frescos of jesus and making him look imprisoned and even sadder. The church was filled with white tourists like us. One wall was amazing, on this shelf-like coffin lay the body of someone holy. It wasn't a real body, though at first I thought it was some saint whose body miraculously did not decompose. It was a mannequin in a royal purple robe, and pinned to every inch of the cloth were prayers in english and spanish, photos of children, small trinkets and coins. Torn pieces of paper inscribed with desperate wishes. I touched my pockets, but I had nothing to offer, and no idea what I would ask for. And plus I couldn't really participate in Catholicism or anything that had male gods. But the wall was really magnificent. I stared at the waxy still face of the holy man. I had no idea who he was. Somewhere in the church Liz and Brad were stealing the collection jar. They scored eight dollars and figured they could really make it big if they came on a Sunday. Leicia was horrified. *It's the catholic church* Liz said with sharp righteousness, and it sounded right.

The tire blew out on the way home. Well, it wasn't that dramatic. It didn't explode, just popped and sagged, and we rode the clunky rim to the shoulder of the road. It was hot like it is in the desert. We were still on the reservation, and the land around us was gouged with mining. Brad changed the tire, heaving the spare from the trunk, spinning the iron X that tightened the nuts. He cut his hand doing it, and it bled. Back in the car, Leicia tapped me quietly and showed me the red splotch on her hand. Brad was HIV+. Its OK, I assured her. You're Fine.

Me and Liz had that book, *The Courage To Heal*. We were obsessed with it, we studied it. You know how people turn to religion in times of crisis. I needed dogma, something solid and sure. There's that whole part of *The Courage To Heal* that says maybe you were molested but you blocked it out and that's why you're so fucked up right now. That was our favorite part. Liz would try to convince people they had been molested, going over the checklist at the front of the book: Do you have nightmares Are you afraid of sex Promiscuous Argumentative Overly-Passive? At the time it did explain everything. I mean, everyone's fucked up and men, who can trust them. Who knows what we've been through. Anything was possible with my stepfather's eye at my door. I had had another father when I was younger, different, named Dennis. There was Liz and that book and me so deranged and suddenly I knew he'd molested me. I couldn't remember anything, I just knew it. He was such an ass-hole, that I remembered. Not a nice man. Actually, he was kind of like Liz — moody, unpredictable, manipula-tive. Liz said that if I thought he may have molested me then he did, why else would I have thought it? She was insistent. Any argument was denial and it meant my path to becoming whole again would be even longer. I had to Heal. I sat with that book on my lap, in the cac-tus yard, in my bed, on the broken couch in the living room, a glass of mezcal sweating on the floor by my feet. Well sure, why not. There were these things. That song *Miracles* by Jefferson Airplane just terrified me. I was little, with my father at a bar. It was daylight out-side but inside was the eternal dusk of the drunk. There was a jukebox, he played that song and I was crawling under one of the booths that lined the wall, grasping onto the table leg and screaming. I was so scared. My father, crouching, trying to pull me out. It was his favorite song. I heard it again when I was a little older and it came on Uncle Charlie's radio and I ran and hid. What did it mean. *It means he molested you!* Liz said, exasperated. I asked my mother about it. *He used to sit in the bedroom with all the lights off and play that song*, she said. *He was weird.*

You've got to start dealing with this Liz insisted. She did not insist gently. It was like dealing was my duty and I was being bad. *You've got to heal!* The fat glossy book on my lap. It's an interesting book, it really is. We loved it all except for the section on prostitution which we conveniently ignored. There's a section on changing your fantasies and that was another thing. Rape fantasies, violent fantasies. *Get a clue Michelle, you were obviously raped!* Liz was so annoyed with me. She had those fantasies too. We began a campaign aimed at getting the violence out of our pussies. The Book offered guidance. One woman wrote down her new, healed fantasy for all the lost perverts to use as inspiration. She is in a boat, in a flowing white dress, she is going to a place that many womyn have journeyed to before. With each lift of the oar she grows more and more aroused. Finally she is there: the sacred island. There is a rock, worn with the bodies of many womyn. She places her body upon it, beneath a shaft of bamboo which trickles water onto her clitoris. Climax. I tried, I really did, but a menacing figure kept sliding out from the trees and clamping a gloved hand over the poor, unsuspecting womyn. Climax.

Another section of The Book was Confronting Your Abuser. Confront your abuser. I didn't even know where he was. Not my stepfather, he was back in Boston, properly confronted, depressed and suicidal. You'd think that would be enough, but more drama was required. I tried to find my father. The last time I saw him was years ago at a 24 hour truck stop me and my friends would masochistically eat at to amuse the truckers with our hairdos. My father was there. I hadn't seen him since before I started high school; he had moved, changed his number, been fired from his job at the post office, possibly for drugs. For a while he was pumping gas near my house but then he was gone. My mother had pulled up to the pump in the new car her new husband had bought for her. That must have felt rich. Then there he was again, drunk at the breakfast counter in a shiny green Celtics jacket. You have to understand the scene my friends made when we walked into this place. We were punks — goth, actually — it was a truck stop, 3 o'clock in the morning, we were ordering BLTs and cokes. Oh My God You Guys — That's My Father! The One Staring In The Celtics Jacket. My friends were very interested. It was kind of legend that my father abandoned me, very 1980s after-school special. I think I got a certain respect for it and they were all amazed that they were getting to see him. He came right up to our table and sat down next to me. He was drunk and thought he was funny, his friends were up at the counter, laughing at Dennis going over to the freaks. He asked us our names, it was pretty unbelievable. Michelle, I said. I had bright pink hair, lots of eyeliner. I was about 16. *Dennis* he said, and held out his hand for me to shake. He was missing a pinkie, it got cut off by a machine in a factory he worked at before I was born. It was a little pink stump at the end of his hand. I shook it, what else could I do. He turned to Peter. *And who're you, Boy George?* He kept calling Rachel Marcia. He eventually left and I guess I ate my BLT. *Bye Bye Boy George* he yelled when we left, still at the counter in his green Celtics jacket. *He knew it was you,* my mother insisted when I told her the story. *There's no way in hell he didn't know who you were.* But he was drunk. Michelle, I said as I shook his hand, and he didn't even flinch.

I heard he moved to Florida. His cousin Irving had been the janitor at my high school, a really nice guy. I think he felt bad for me and my broken home, he was always offering me a dollar for lunch. Irving had a daughter Ellie, a little older than me, she was trouble. She had a slutty reputation and a lot of eyeliner. She tried to kill herself in 9th grade by eating a bottle of aspirin, they had to pump her stomach. Irving was a frustrated hairdresser, he had gone to beauty school, in retrospect maybe he was gay. Not to enforce stereotypes. Irving would stop me in the halls to ask about my hair, how did I get it like that, was it a double-process, what I could do to keep it healthy. He saw my father right before he went south, at the funeral of some obscure aunt I never knew. *She's a good kid* Irving told him. *You should call before you go. She don't hold a grudge.* Irving was sweet but he didn't know shit. I wore grudges for underwear.

My father hated most of his family. He had all these brothers and they all just detested each other. Henry was the only brother he spoke to, the only piece of my father's family I actually knew. We went to barbecues in the grassy space of the housing projects he lived in. It was scary to me, the thought of living in those uniform buildings. They were all the same, how could you remember which one you lived in. Years later Henry still lived there. I found his phone number easily, I called him up. I wanted my father's phone number. Henry was uneasy. *He might not want you to have it* he said, *I have to ask.* He called me back at my little cactus home in Tucson. *Why don't you give me your number,* he said. *He wants to call you.* The next day the phone rang. Brad walked into the gold bedroom. He had asked who it was and the voice said *Her Father. Which one* snapped Brad, and I love him for that. *How you doin' sweetheart* said

157

the long lost Dad. I hadn't heard that voice forever. It sounded like sludge. I'm not being dramatic, he really did have the voice of a monster. He used to cough all the time, thick phlegm he spat into toilet paper and left around the house for me and my mother to clean up. These crusty white balls, I'd pinch them with the tips of my fingers and run to the trash can. His voice was like that. I couldn't believe he called me *sweetheart*. The arrogance. I Know That You Sexually Abused Me I said, wasting no time. I Know, And I Want You To Know That I Know. *You're sick* he said in that wet Boston voice, *you're really fucking sick*, and I threw my voice over his saying I Remember I Remember What You Did I Remember Everything. Of course I didn't remember a thing. He hung up on me. I was leaning into the kitchen doorway, my roommates were in the living room, listening with their eyes cast to the floor. Liz was in the bed, stoned, she didn't come out, she didn't hold my hand.

So I thought I might kill my father. I knew, though I did not say this to Liz, that he may not have molested me, but still he was such an asshole and I thought it would be fine if he died. This murder idea came to me months after the phone call, when I was back in Boston and Liz was in Tucson but was still my girlfriend. I was bored. I was hunting my father like a detective or a paid assassin. I was in my crummy hometown of Chelsea, at city hall with a phonebook and a pen. I was matching up addresses with a coffee-stained map of the city. There were a few Swankowskis and they all lived in really crappy parts of town, these neighborhoods that used to be polish but now were just slums. I walked into an old building that sat across from the stretching green of the Tobin

Bridge, cars zooming by on their way to Boston. I was looking for Andrew Swankowski, he was either my uncle or my grandfather. I knocked on a dark wood door, no answer. Up a flight of stairs, moving through the musty smell of a really old place, like all old people lived their with their old furniture and their old, old clothes. I knocked on another door, a little boy answered, he looked at me blankly. I knew it was the wrong apartment but I waited as the mother came to the door, long hair, really out of it. Does Andrew Swankowski Live In This Building? I asked. Do You Know Andrew Swankowski? She shook her head. She was zonked. Up on the third floor an old woman came to her door when I knocked, plump and lively in a housecoat and lipstick. *Oh, Andy's dead, honey. He had sugar, they had to cut his toes off.* Something bizarre like that. *Oh, you're Dennis's daughter, right!* She remembered him vaguely. I think she was just happy to have a visitor. She made me kind of sad, so happy in her hallway with her bright mouth of lipstick, all dressed up in her housecoat. I thanked her and left. Next on my list was cousin Irving the Janitor and he was glad to hear from me. I told him I was trying to find my father. I didn't mention I intended to kill him. This search was really hopeless. My father hated all these people, he'd never stay in touch. Irving was indignant. *A kid's got a right to talk to her father,* he said. *You call Henry he'll know.* Henry Won't Give Me His Number, I said. *You tell him to give it to you or I'll kick his ass.* I thought about stealing Henry's mail, his phone bill would certainly have my father's number on it. I'd find out where he was, the state, the city, I could stalk him. He'd be easy to find, he was a drunk. I'd hang out in bars, watching. Liz would

159

put on the 200 dollar blonde wig she wore to whore, she would get all femmed up with lipstick and one of her silky cleavage dresses, she would seduce my drunk father into an alley and I would be waiting there with a knife. There was a point in time where I really could have done this. After doing so much activism I had decided it was all catharsis, futile, and if I really wanted to make a difference I should just start blowing things up and killing men. And then Liz's letters from Tucson started drifting in, flowery script about herbs, meditation and nutrition. Men were eating too much bleached flour and that's why they act violently. Get the men off the white bread and everything will be fine. Liz was letting go of her anger. It was like hearing she got a new girlfriend, I felt so betrayed. My anger was tight in my pocket and it was the only thing keeping me on the earth. I would find Dennis Swankowski and I would kill him alone. I didn't need Liz and her wig. I didn't even need a knife or a gun, I had my hands and my hot, hot anger. But the time wasn't right, not then, not yet. I hunted and I hunted but I couldn't track my father down.

* ★ *

Ok let me tell you how I ended up whoring again in Tucson even though the deal was Liz would support our life in the desert, to make up for all the work I did in Boston to bring us there. Liz had a series of visions. She had a vision of her recently dead grandfather's penis bobbing before her, and she remembered that she had been raped by him from infancy until age eighteen. I felt a sick relief hearing her say this, barging into our bedroom where I had been trying to take some time alone, reading my tarot cards, just lying around the way Liz always did. It seemed to keep her so content with herself and I figured I could use some self-contentment, since at this point I was a definite wreck, waking each morning with a rumbling diarrhea that brought me in and out of the bathroom all day long, my chest an accompanying video game of laserlike panic and cramps. My attempts at Calm were fading, but Liz's sudden revelation of rape brightened me, gave me a shot of hope that maybe now everything would be alright. We had a culprit. Surely this was why Liz was such an incredible bitch, and understanding this would change everything and we could finally be lesbians in love the way I'd wanted. These recovered memories placed Liz at the starting point of the Emergency Stage, as talked about in *The Courage To Heal*. *I'm in the emergency stage*, she told me. *I need to remove everything stressful from my life.* Sex was stressful, provoking images of the bobbing penis and its removal was barely noticeable. And Liz had also already removed herself emotionally, but now she had the banner of Abuse to wrap around her absence. Any talk about our relationship interfered with her healing process. My healing process interfered with her healing process. Liz no longer wanted to hear about my stepfather's sick voyeurism, my suicidal mother or my lost, hysterical sister. She had her own victim drama and no longer had to live vicariously through my abuse. Whoring was interfering with her healing process and I would have to go to work for us. But I'm Still In The Emergency Stage Too, I protested. But my abuse hadn't been physical, I was not haunted by images of trespassing cocks, I could better handle seeing the men. It didn't even occur to either of us to get a normal job. That's not what we were doing right then. Within a week I had a beeper, a new job, and a new name — Tiffany. I worked four days a week, I cooked food for Liz, ran to the co-op to find herbal remedies to settle her aching stomach, gave her money to fill the bowl of her bong. It's like she was dying. She just lay there on the futon, occasionally leaving for solitary trips to the desert, returning to eat the stir fry I'd made. I was Liz's girlfriend. I told her to take her time and heal, and I would get us through this. Taking my tiny revenges wherever I could find them, I began to steal from my tricks. I liked bringing the objects home like trophies to show to Liz, to our friends. It was like taking something back from a dream, to go to this other place that none of them understood and return with a keepsake or a twisted souvenir. I wasn't out for the glitzy, expensive items, though of course they were satisfying. I took what was most easily snatched. A toothbrush, clear purple plastic, brand new in its windowed package. It was the only thing in the bathroom. I was at some guy's guest house, not lived in and barely furnished. A tall, gangly, red-haired guy who was in a band. The living room held big black amps and coils of rubbery wire, and gleaming guitars set on their stands like small kings. To steal one of those, impossible. I had the toothbrush squished into my handbag, the awkward plastic wrapping crinkling against the tin tube of lube, the delicate squares of condoms. I was afraid it would force open the purse's single weak snap and tumble out onto the floor, a nightmare. The guys all thought you were desperate to start with, how horrible to get caught lifting a toothbrush. I got it home and gave it to Liz, whose toothbrush was a fluffy explosion of bristles spent from so much brushing.

Liz had perfect teeth, straight and white as her Connecticut upbringing that held dentistry to be a necessity, not the luxury it was for my family.

I remember stealing from a narrow closet a handful of thin red candles. Their wicks were long and charred and it felt kind of gross to take them, like trashpicking, but it was the only thing that would fit in my purse. I really should have invested in a roomier bag, one of Liz's big cloth sacks from Guatemala, but they weren't glamorous enough to accompany a prostitute. I swiped a big jar of cold cream from someone's medicine cabinet, Clinique. It was fat and expensive and I felt a murky joy imagining the trick's wife searching the small, brightly-lit bathroom, rummaging through drawers, asking *honey, have you seen my cleanser?* I didn't ever use the cold cream, an ocean of greasy white discolored here and there with smears of black mascara, blue eyeshadow. It was too gross. The jar sat in my bathroom like a tank in a meadow, neighbors with Liz's jasmine massage oil, spiny stalks of aloe clipped from our yard, Brad's sweet-smelling hair goo in the pretty blue bottle. Clinique, like a billboard in our bathroom, advertising a culture we would not participate in.

One trick left me alone for a moment so he could answer his phone, and I snatched a snapshot right from his living room mantle. It really is amazing how safe men feel; to let a perfect stranger into their home — one involved in a disreputable and illegal profession — and feel no fear for their safety or their possessions or anything. It infuriated me. If they knew how hot my heart burned with hate for them they'd have been scared. The picture I stole showed the guy and his girlfriend smiling brilliant white smiles, done up all fancy at some big function. He had a really weird body; he had been a bodybuilder but then stopped working out, so his muscles hung like jelly sacs from his body and he looked really freakish. The photo fit easily in my purse and I was glad to have scored something of obvious sentimental value.

I stole a candle, a really nice one. One of those round candles with bright, kaleidoscopic wax. I had complimented it and the trick told me it was a gift from his daughter. She was predictably blonde; professional portraits of her hung in every hall of the house. The trick was this really old guy with Parkinson's Disease and it had to be one of the worst calls ever. He shook violently and more than once nearly toppled over onto the linoleum. He couldn't get hard. He had me lie on the kitchen table on a mangy fake fur rug while he rubbed talcum powder onto my body with his awful trembling hands. You would think I'd have been glad to not have to fuck him, but it was almost worse. The TV was on at a terrible volume, Wheel Of Fortune, and there was this teensy excited dog running in circles around the house, barking a shrill incessant bark. *Shut up, shut up dog* the trick kept yelling in his jerky voice and I bet if I wasn't there he would've kicked it. I felt no compassion for this pathetic, shivering man because I knew he was an asshole. You could see it; a macho arrogance that struggled to push through the veiny web of helplessness his disease had wrapped him in. I figured it was probably karma. He got me a can of generic coke from the fridge and insisted on opening it even though it took forever with his shoddy motor skills. I just thought the whole time about that beautiful round candle and how it would never fit in my purse. There was a knick-knack I could've grabbed easy, a tiny replica of a southwestern mission, brass and copper with lacy patches of patina like lichen. It was definitely worth more but it was the candle I wanted, that globe of fractured color. I wrapped it in my sweater and hoped for the best. That really was the worst call. My pimp/madam/"agent" Katarina had warned me to get the money up front since he tended not to have it and of course I forgot and of course he did not have the money. I wanted to kill him. It had occurred to me numerous times during the hour, how easy it would be to knock him over and leave him twitching on the floor like a big wrinkled fish while I ransacked his apartment. Really, more than the candle I wanted to steal his dog. You could tell he didn't love it and it really seemed to like me, hopped all over me while I sat on the couch drinking my generic cola. I thought it would be neat to have a little kidnapped dog.

We had to drive the trick to the bank in Liz's car. It was unbelievable. I don't drive. Harold, the little trust fund mooch who, along with Liz's brother Jeremy, was crashing at my house and living off my earnings, was attempting to pay part of his rent by chauffeuring me around to my calls. He pulled the car up to the beautiful house in the foothills of the desert, gorgeous blooming cactuses and languid mesquite trees drooping their thorny branches, and there I was with grandpa, playing the bitchy whore to the hilt. The hour was up and I didn't have to be nice to him anymore. Get In The Car I growled and we waited forever as he navigated his sputtering body into the front seat. I tossed my sweater in the back and it landed with a thud, heavy with the weight of my candle. Harold had to escort the trick into the bank, holding his sick body like a crutch, walking him carefully through the glass doors. It pissed me off to watch Harold handle him so carefully, almost tenderly. He hadn't had to lay naked on the matted hide of a skinned stuffed animal while the creep massaged him with baby powder. Certainly Harold would never find himself in a situation anything like that. I hated them both. The story, in case any of the bank people inquired, was that Harold was the trick's nephew, and I thought that was very appropriate. Since I could not fathomably pass for any branch of the family tree, I waited in the hot car and fondled my candle. It was really pretty.

Harold brought the guy back into his house while I stayed in the tiled front yard and played with the dog. Harold, I Want The Dog I whispered when he came back out. *Michelle, you can't* he said. Harold thought I was crazy. He was so arrogant. He was acting like since he had had to touch the trick he had somehow participated in the call and deserved a bit of my money. You're Earning Your Keep Harold, I gently reminded him. You're Living In My House For Free. *Well can you at least buy me a smoothie?*

I gave the candle to our new friend Julisa because it went with the eclectic decor of her adobe. She kept it lit by her bed and each time I visited it was softer, a ball of slowly melting color. I thought it would be cool to do some kind of art exhibit with all my stolen trophies, but I wasn't an artist and Liz and I never did start our art gallery, so it never happened.

* ★ *

It was the eve of our departure from Tucson and I was at Julisa's house, hiding from my pimp. Being very dramatic about it, enjoying it, actually. If we do plot our existences in the space between death and life than I did a good job with this one. Really keeping myself on my earthly toes. Now that we had really settled into Tucson, made some friends, painted our kitchen with red and yellow paint, hung a string of chilies in our window, established some semblance of Home, Liz decided it was time to leave. We would go back to the east coast and spend the summer in Provincetown. Liz always had a plan. I think it's because she drove, and owned a car. I didn't have a car and had never learned how to drive and I could not come up with a plan I believed in. I would go with Liz. It would be nice, I thought, to be by the ocean again. To be close to Boston, a place I understood and could get around in, in case I had to break up with Liz again.

Julisa's house — my hideout that last night — was behind ours, and if I stood on her little porch with the hammock and the scroungy old couch I could see light from our windows and the shadows of people packing up my things. They would phone occasionally with updates. *Katarina called, she's concerned, you didn't show up for your call at the Travel Lodge, the guy's annoyed, he's still waiting for you.* Fifteen minutes later, *Katarina called again, she's confused, she said you paged her with the 'arrival' code but you're not at the hotel, why did you do that, now she knows something's weird.* I had dialed up Katarina The Pimp's beeper and punched in the numbers that meant I had arrived safe and sound at my call when really I was sprawled restless on a futon and the john was fuming and pitching a fit. I was just bored to tears and felt ripped off because I had caused this big commotion and couldn't even enjoy it because I was sequestered away in case she came to the house looking for me. My pimp was going crazy and my friends were having all the fun taking her phone calls while I sat in this house of stillness and calm. Even the cats were mellow. Dim light from the lamp washed over the carpet and Julisa's many possessions — rocks, CDs, dried flowers, all kinds of things hanging on the walls. Most people keep the proof of their history in a box or a drawer but Julisa pinned hers to every part of her house so you knew all about her the minute you walked in. The phone rang again and I answered it, my big fun. Katarina's really frantic now and Brad yelled at her and said *nothing better have happened to her, you better find her* and so Katarina is driving around Tucson in her fancy car looking for me. They were all excited, my friends, putting stuff into boxes, probably stoned or maybe drinking wine. Hoping that Katarina would come to the house so they could see her. She looked young and pretty but it was all surgery. Katarina would leave messages on my voice mail like *Oh you'll like this one, he's real sweet* or *he's real funny* or *he's real good looking*, and I'd save them so my friends could call and listen to them. The best one was the warning she left me about the guy with the inflatable penis who had to spend five minutes in the hotel bathroom pumping it up like a balloon in the Macy's parade. My friends in Tucson were healthy, natural types, kind of hippieish, political about the

168

earth. They had met us at an animal rights demonstration — me, Liz and Brad, three whores from the east coast who talked fast and caused loud trouble and these hippie girls adored us. We had made their life a movie for three months and this was the climax, the big chase scene. I had arranged to meet Katarina at the Texaco on Speedway immediately following the Travel Lodge call I never went to. I was supposed to drop off her cut of the money, about three hundred dollars. That I would not show up was my farewell fuck you. Katarina was an idiot. What did she say that time, *I don't know why feminists get upset, if all men were like the men we deal with everything would be great!* She thought they were all nice guys. Katarina was far beyond the general low standards straight women have for men. All my worst calls came from her agency, 'Classy Lady' I think it was called. Tucson apartment complex trash. This guy with the filthiest place, no air in there but cigarette smoke and shit stained underwear in the bathroom. Another repulsive little man wanting me to crap on him and I tried but all that came was urine. He wanted to make a date with me for when I had my period. The house was this little shack with covered windows that made me think of *Silence of the Lambs*. I made Liz and Brad wait outside the whole time and Brad ended up getting in a fight with the next door neighbor and the trick heard the commotion and freaked out, came and got me in the shower where I was rinsing the pee off my legs, saying *you've got to go right now!* I would tell Katarina about these calls and she would act so offended, this prissy outrage. *Well, that is unacceptable. That is just awful. We won't see him again. If*

*anyone wants you to pee or anything you just leave,
we don't do that.* When she hired me she told me plainly
that we don't do blow jobs. It was because the condoms
taste so yucky and plus it's not very becoming. Katarina
was the most ladylike pimp-slash-prostitute I'd ever
met. Practically uptight, nearing prudishness. Her apartment was this very sterile southwestern. She had all the
stuff but somehow the culture was not present. Earlier
that day had been the very worst call, this jocky red-
meat guy who kept trying to send me away to come
back in ten or fifteen minutes and I had been dropped
off, was essentially stranded in one of Tucson's residen-
tial hells, long stretches of awful homes going on forever, with only highways and hot air in between. Finally
he let me in and what was the problem, his girlfriend
was there, that's what he was saying but I saw the
woman leave and I knew she was a whore. Probably he
called a couple places and it was first come first served
and he tried to get me to leave again, after I had wan-
dered through the suburbs and then sat in his living
room while he finished his time with his 'girlfriend'. I
was so annoyed. I flipped through a flashy porn mag
that had been left (for me?) on the couch, trying to dis-
tract myself from the blaring television that I couldn't
figure out how to turn off and also the maniacally barking dog that was freaking out on the patio, pushing its
furry face up against the sliding glass doors, drooling. It
was a rabid monster and I couldn't stop imagining it
breaking the glass and coming after me.

The jock took forever. I was hanging out in suburbia in heels and a dress and was feeling increasingly
bitchy. Finally he came out, his whore 'girlfriend' trot-

ting out before him in killer heels and a tight skirt. She gave me the whore solidarity look, I saw it, a quick shift of her heavily mascarad eyes and a little smirk at her mouth. I smiled back. She left the house and the jock came back in with the announcement that he wasn't going to pay me and I should go. This being the big night when I had planned to blow Katarina off and keep her cut, and I was wanting lots of money. And jock boy said he changed his mind and I should just leave and since we didn't do anything he wasn't going to pay me. You Pay Me For My Time, I snapped, and we started arguing and I called Katarina. She had me put him on the phone and I guess she threatened him, made references to nonexistent thugs being sent to his house or something. It is funny to imagine prim Katarina threatening violence, but it worked. The jock went back into his room for the money and I stayed on the phone with Katarina, she was saying things like *Are you OK He's an asshole Take the money and get right out of there*. She was being very nice and capable and I felt a little bad about my plan to rip her off, but only just a little. The jock kicked his way back into the living room and tossed me the money. He was steaming, yelling at me to get out of his house and I was being calm, I had this cordless phone in my hand with Katarina on the other end and I told him I was going to bring the phone to the door and I did, walking kind of sideways so I could keep my eye on him because he was very angry and though I can't at all remember what he looked like I imagine it was red. I remember saying into the phone He's Getting Violent but I don't think he was, it just seemed very close. He was telling me he was going to call the cops.

Go Ahead, You Called A Prostitute, Go Call The Cops And See If They Help You. It was fast, a bright flash, the journey down his hall. At the door he ripped the phone from my hand and hung up on Katarina's tinny voice. He pushed me outside, slammed the door. I was breathing. I had my money, I was OK, I was breathing. I didn't have to fuck him. I was waiting for my ride in front of his house which the cops may or may not be on their way to. I dumped my condoms and KY behind some neatly trimmed suburban hedges. Cops can use that against you, log it in as evidence. I was creating a whole story in my head, I had a date with the jock but when I got to his house he had another woman there and he got nervous and told her I was a prostitute, which of course made me very angry, and we had a fight and he got violent and threw me out. He was a guy I met at a nightclub. Which nightclub. Where do straight people go in Tucson. He seemed nice and he asked me out on a date. It was outrageous I know. I was freaking out. I knew I looked like a nice girl, kind of young, I thought that would maybe save me. The cops never came. Katarina came, scaring the hell out of me by driving up onto the curb in her slick little car, her headlights seizing me up like a rabbit. I climbed into the front and sat there with her. I was pretty shaky. She asked if I had her cut from the calls I did earlier and I said no though I really did, all rolled up in my shoe in case the cops had come and searched my purse. I sat in Katarina's car until my ride came. I went home. Everyone was there, packing up the house. We were going back to Boston. Julisa had her video camera, she was filming a documentary about us because our lives were so interesting. I told them what happened, told it to the camera. I guess it was the final scene. They picked me up at Julisa's house around two in the morning. I had eventually just fallen asleep on the futon. Katarina had quit calling and now we had some money for the road. I slept in the back seat with pillows on the boxes until we stopped in Flagstaff with the sun coming up and got a hotel.

Nowhere Left To Go
Boston, Provincetown and Tucson, 1992

It was pretty horrible to land in Boston and crawl, unwanted, back to the floor of Teri's Jamaica Plain flat, to sleep and argue and try again to start fresh in a new place with Liz. We moved around so much, every time a new home came into view through the window I looked out on a city of hope, a place where it could be good. Teri's floor was hell. It was like we failed at something, like we went out into the world and the world kicked us out, sent us back to tired Boston. Just for a month or so, Liz promised Teri, who was too nice to kick us out into the street. We truly had no place else to go. We gave her the string of chilies that had been in our kitchen window, proof that we had really been somewhere. We drove into Provincetown that winter, to hunt an apartment. It was already well into the summer tourist season — all the places Liz had hoped to find a room at were full. I felt old pushing through crowded Commercial Street; I hadn't been there since I was happy. We found a grey little room in a building that faced the town's hyperactive main street, we paid our first installment and lugged our futon up the stairs. The place had a communal patio, and that's where we were on the fourth of July, standing around with all the other roomers, watching the fireworks. The house was really a boarding house, practically

174

a hotel. It seemed like everyone in Provincetown lived in one, like no one had an actual apartment. Each summer the town becomes flooded with transient alcoholics, people who work the tourist shops all day and drink booze all night in small wooden bars hung with glass balls and fishing nets. Finally stumbling down the town's main street to these one room living spaces with no kitchens and communal bathrooms. This one was one of the better ones, it had the big porch that looked onto Commercial Street. You could sit outside when your room got too stuffy, grill some vegetables on the rusty Hibachi. That's where we were as the fireworks exploded over the harbor, their lights flashing on the fishing boats bobbing at the shore. The boys were straight and drunk, sucking the last bits of foam from their bottles, trying to organize another beer run. Betsy who owned the place had brought her dog, an emaciated greyhound who got spooked each time the sky burst, whining and weaving through the patio furniture. I was watching for his startled reaction at each detonation. I poked Liz. Watch The Dog. She rolled her eyes angrily. *He's scared! This is totally unnatural, blowing things up in the sky! What the fuck! It's falling into the ocean, it's fucking pollution!* Liz was really something. She'd been a mean little troublemaker her whole life but getting a political consciousness had really given her direction. I'd watched her progress from random cruelty to truly righteous hostility. She hated the fireworks and hated us for being stupid enough to enjoy them. *Why don't you try looking at the moon* instead she snapped. It was full that night, hung in the sky like a supporting actress. Gerry the dyke who lived downstairs was there as well, and Liz had a special hatred for her because she worked at a leather store and also because I had given her the fat pink armchair that came with our room. Gerry had come up one day to introduce herself in a neighborly fashion, and her eyes had locked on the chair and since I never sat in it I helped her carry it downstairs to her room, chipping wood from the stairway as we struggled to keep it steady. About two weeks after we lugged all our shit out to the Cape Liz announced she was going back to Tucson. Alone. We weren't breaking up, Liz just needed Space, we spent all our Time together, how did we know who we were? It is true that I did not know who I was. It is true that I didn't know anything. I knew that Liz was my girlfriend and that everything was awful and if her going away could make it better then I would stay behind, work on my own shit, and we would meet in the desert at the end of the summer, two new people. I liked the idea of that little room in Provincetown as my own apartment. It was kind of an amazing idea. I thought about what I could do to it. I gave Gerry the armchair and as it happened Liz just loved that chair, and had really been looking forward to spending the rest of her time on Cape Cod sitting in it and smoking pot til she was too stoned to stand back up. We had an enormous fight. She wanted to break up right there. It was a space issue, she had no fucking space of her own. It was true, she didn't. I had taken the little room over, giving away the fat armchair and turning the table into an altar covered with seashells and candles and a silver goblet filled with ocean water and lacy green algae. Liz was so angry. We didn't break up but she refused to acknowledge that the table had become an altar and she'd leave her shit all over it — coffee cups and pot and crusty band-aids from the blisters her new Tevas were giving her. And so Liz hated Gerry, because the fat pink armchair was hers now and she was really into the fireworks, holding a cigarette to her lips as she looked out at the sky.

After the fireworks Liz and I walked to Cafe Euro, an overpriced, touristy place we could afford because we both were prostitutes again, working every other week at Lyn's in-call back in the city. She had been happy to hear from us again, and anxious to put us to work. Cafe Euro had live reggae on weekends, in a back room that was big as a ballroom, with a huge paper mache mermaid reaching out from the wall. The people there were well into being drunk, hopping around and spinning to the music. As far as I could tell they were all straight. Provincetown is a big gay vacation spot but we never went to the gay bars because we were now in this psychotically feminist state where absolutely everything offended us. Drag queens, S/M, miniskirts. I had sold all my objectifying clothing back in Tucson, and was wearing some flouncy indian number belonging to Liz, very hippie and comfortable. The bartender that night was this straight boy who lived in the room across from ours. Just last week he had stumbled into my room, late, on all kinds of drugs, thinking he was in the bathroom. He was naked and the big challenge was to guide him back out before he pissed on my floor. That night, however, he was both fully clothed and sober. He noticed our entrance and waved us over to the bar, fixed us a couple of drinks for free. I can't remember his name but he looked like, what's his name, that guy from the New York Dolls. Buster Poindexter, but that's not his real name either. The boy behind the bar had that kind of face, real babyish but also real butch. Like a hound dog. Like I could understand women finding him attractive even though I found him repulsive. I had drunk beer with him on the porch a few weeks ago. I had been grilling tofu, it kept slipping off the skewers into the charcoal, and he came out with some bottles and cigarettes and I started drinking his alcohol and smoking his cigarettes and then he brought out a joint dipped in hash oil and we smoked it and I started steering the conversation towards things like pornography so I could know whether or not to hate him. Mostly he was just dumb. We ended up arguing about if Robert Crumb is sexist. I was telling Liz about this as the boy worked on our drinks, because I thought she wanted to sleep with him. I was telling her he flunked all the tests, he was a Bad Man, but she kept looking at him. It seems all my stories about Liz culmi-nate with some activity around a man. She was so not a dyke. I don't know what she got out of being with me, a girl. Maybe a rest. Or she was trying to align her life with her newfound politics. Either way she was missing the boys. She watched the bartender with the focus of the stoned, this glazed stare and a little smirk on her face. I grabbed my vodka drink from the bar and started sucking on the straw, watched the white people trying to dance to another Bob Marley cover. Liz and the bar-tender talked until the bar got too crowded and the two of us moved across the room and sat in the shadow of the paper mache mermaid. I wanted to make out, be in her face, but Liz wasn't into public displays of affection. We sat and drank and tried to talk over the band, stuff about What Is Sex And What Is Love, What Is Real And

What Comes From Society And Your Parents. I just kept sucking at my vodka, feeling it splash cold in my stomach. I hated the whole conversation. She just wanted to fuck that boy and she turned it into some theoretical discussion, framing me as the co-dependent lesbian girlfriend. Which I was. It escalated and I stormed out of the dancehall, crying down Commercial Street to the bass beat of house music leaking from the gay bars. Pushing through the drunk white tourists. If she went home with him and fucked him I would hear it. He lived right across the hall, I heard it when he played his music, the same Lemonheads CD over and over and over. I could hear it when his alcoholic friends came over and drank beer and talked bullshit. I didn't want to go back to the room. It smelled like musty sea and marijuana and the eucalyptus oil we smeared on the cat to scare off the fleas. I could see the ocean hiding behind the shops as I passed, thin stripes that moved and glinted darkly. It ran alongside Commercial Street like a highway. It was the most poetic and most obvious place to go so I went there. To look at the big hanging moon that none of the humans appreciated. It had stayed in the sky til the fireworks burned out and now it had the place to itself. I walked through a parking lot til my feet hit sand, ducked under someone's porch and hopped onto a concrete block that was planted on the shore. I sat there and cried at the neglected moon and thought about being in love with a vacationing straight girl that I had left my entire life for. I didn't even have my own clothes anymore, just all these cotton things that were too big for me. I was crying and wishing for a cigarette and the tide was slowly coming in around my little perch and I realized if I didn't leave soon I'd be trapped by the ocean. I hopped down and waded back to the parking lot. I thought about getting another drink, then thought about my mother saying drinking alone is the surest sign of alcoholism. I walked across the street to the rooming house. Liz was in bed with the cat. She lay on her back with her eyes open, breasts falling to the sides of her chest. I crawled in beside her. I'm Sorry I said. I didn't know what I was apologizing for. I just wanted everything to be OK.

OK, so this plan, Liz leaving for the desert again, me left in Provincetown, our proposed reunion in the desert come October with some vague idea of living in a tent and being self-sufficient, this was an exercise in being alone. Independent. Except Liz was in that rich warm place with the hot pink sky and all our new friends, and I was remaining in the place I'd always been. We'd been together for more than a year and she took the life we'd been sharing when she left. I had this small damp room and the cat she left behind, I had the whore job in Boston that was making me crazy. I took the ferry back and forth across the harbor, out of my mind lonely. She sent me letters on thin sheets of handmade paper stamped with Hindu designs. How she was getting to know herself better in my absence, through going to sweat lodges and pot lucks and camping trips with all our friends who by the way say Hi and hope I'm having fun by the ocean. Those letters depressed the hell out of me. I was failing the independence exercise. I would read her words alone in my chilly room, feeling more and more cut off from anything that was mine, finally rushing across the street to the pay phone in the parking lot to call her in the throes of a panic attack. Watching the small wooden fishing boats bobbing in the harbor. I'm Having A Hard Time With This, I said. *It's OK* she soothed in her soft, stoned voice. Liz was always very nice when we were apart. It made me forget about what a mean bitch she was when we were together. I was full of fear and loneliness weaved with the injustice that I had given her the money to take herself west and lie in the sun while I stayed where I was and kept whoring. And the terrible idea that I had centered my life on this woman who didn't really care about me and it was my own damn fault and I'd built my shoddy boat and now I was going to drown in it. But the being alone was bigger. I Miss You, I said, an admission of defeat. I'm Not Going To Make It To October. I'm Going Crazy Here. *Well, Brad's coming*, she said. *I just spoke to him. He got a drive-away car, we talked about you maybe driving out with him.* You Did? *I guess it'd be alright.* Yeah, I said. I Mean, We Can Still Spend A Lot Of Time Apart. I had my stuff in boxes immediately, lugging them barefoot to the post office, shipping them out to the desert. I was avoiding Betsy the landlord like never before. Whenever she saw me she'd give me a warning about my second rent payment coming up. On the day I escaped I was smuggling my stuff past her porch. Like all slumlords, her own personal living space was considerably nicer than those of her tenants. I could see her through the sliding-glass doors, fixing mimosas in the kitchen. Bye-bye Betsy I chuckled. I left her a note on the rickety white bureau that came with the room: Sorry to skip out on the rent, but you're really not a very nice person.

The drive-away car was a shiny new Infinity belonging to some frat boy at the U of A. It was a real score. You never know what those drive-away companies are going to send you. This one had a loud, clear stereo and a radar detector perched on the sunvisor like a guardian angel. Brad was in the driver's seat listening to Morrissey. I do not know how to drive. I sat beside him and passed him water, checked on Liz's cat, a nervous ball of fur named Pal. Riding in cars was really too much for Pal. He wouldn't get out of his litter box. He'd darken the gravel with urine, lie down in it and cry. I think he was having a kitty-cat nervous breakdown. I felt very close to him. Oh, Pal, I Know, I Know. I patted his little black head. I did not feel freed, I felt like someone institutionalized being moved to a more privileged dormitory. I sat in the car as it moved out of Massachusetts, trying to figure out exactly how I lost control of my life. Pal howled. Life Is Crazy, I said, and blew pot smoke in his face to calm him down. He loved it, pushed his slanty little face right into the cloud. *I'm worried about him,* Brad said looking over his shoulder. *He's lying in his own piss.* At Least He's Not Moving I said. Whenever Pal moved he left a trail of tiny pinpricks in the pristine leather interior. He was such a scared little animal, his claws were out the whole time, curved and waiting to cling. Oh, Pal, I Know, I Know. Brad and I had a three hundred dollar deposit down on that car and I watched it shrink each time Pal's paw came down.

Brad decided that to make maximum time we should drive til 4 o'clock in the morning. We drank styrofoam towers of truck stop coffee. I read to him by the overhead light, anthologies documenting the gay, lesbian and bisexual struggle. He told me about being at a bar the other night and this straight couple tried to pick him up. They kept buying him drinks. *They were married,* he said. *I kissed a married woman.* You Kissed The Woman? Yeah. Well, What Did You Think? *It was kind of fun*, he said, *but I wasn't really into it.* I thought about all the boys I'd ever claimed to like and came up with two that I actually had some kind of attraction to — Adam, who had long curly hair and wore eyeliner, and Zane, who was homeless and sliced his chest with razors. I was telling this to Brad when we passed a sign announcing exits for the towns Adams and Zane. Oh My God That's So Weird! What Does That Mean? That night we slept in a chilly Howard Johnson's and I dreamt that I arrived in Tucson and Liz had a boyfriend but wanted me for a girlfriend too. Brad dreamt his father had a knife and was trying to kill him. I heard him gasping in his sleep and climbed into his bed to shake him awake.

We stopped one night in Texas. Hereford, Texas, like the Hereford cow. The cops had cow patches on their jackets and the air itself seemed a product of cow shit. We got a room at the Camelot, giant burned-out sign arcing over dingy blue bungalows. Brad rang the service bell and a man rose, half-asleep, from the floor behind the counter. I hid in the car and we split the single-occupancy rent. We locked Pal in the room and drove down the road to the all-night grocery store. Brad was bleary. Wet Paint Wet Paint Watch Out! I yelled as Brad pulled the bumper into the freshly painted parking pole. A sticky yellow smear drying quickly on the frat boy's new Infinity. I watched our deposit evaporate. The grocery store had a deli with a greasy-skinned woman who fixed us grilled cheeses. We took them back to the Camelot with a bottle of Boone's sangria, settled down with our stinky food and got our first good look at the room. It

183

was repulsive. There were cigarettes mashed into the linoleum in the bathroom and the carpet around the bed was stained and somewhat damp. Pal was entertaining himself with a half-dead roach in the corner. Oh Brad, Look 1 said, pulling back the bed's sole blanket. The sheet that wrapped around the mattress was torn and smeared with a suspicious brown matter. Oh, That's Gross. Oh, We Can't Stay Here. We've Got To Get A Different Room, This Is Terrible. Brad left to fight with the drowsy concierge. Brad excels at those types of things — talking to cops, negotiating with authority. He grew up a rich white boy in Connecticut and not even being a faggot can rinse that from your blood. The concierge was angry, he knew that there were two of us and that we had an animal in the room. He tried to hold us responsible for room's filthy condition, but Brad managed to get us a key to the room next door. It was, of course, equally disgusting. Oh, I'm Never Going To Be Able To Sleep In This Place. 1 was whining, drinking sangria. 1 was certain I'd wake up with some terrible skin problem. Brad went out to the car and dug up a bunch of blankets, we lined the skanky bed with them and woke up free of any strange itches or rashes.

Liz was not even there when we arrived. We went directly to Julisa's house, where she was staying. Julisa was there, lying naked on her futon like some voluptuous woman off a museum wall. Round as a bowl of fruit. She pulled me down into a sweaty embrace. *Liz went to the desert for the day.* But She Knew We Were Getting In Today. Julisa shrugged. It was August in Tucson. Monsoon season. You could see them moving in from the mountains, furious clouds split with lightning.

An ambush of rain that would cool the air for about fifteen minutes til the sun came back and dried everything up and you wondered if you just imagined it. Liz came back into town with those clouds rolling behind her. *Hi* she said, real casual, like I was a neighborhood acquaintance dropping by to borrow something. She was wearing Julisa's clothes and a gauzy scarf around her head. That breathy voice, husky with pot. She fixed me a sandwich of fried seaweed and mustard and I sat across from her on Julisa's porch, munching on the ocean. The air was still in Tucson, warm all around you. At night it was delicious, you just moved right through it. I told Liz about my trip. I told her about my dream, how she was fucking this boy but wanted me too. She had these eyes that were blue and hard, not water but ice. Blue like a sled dog. Deceptively clear. *You are a very psychic woman* she said, and told me about her boyfriend.

SEMIOTEXT(E) · NATIVE AGENTS SERIES
Chris Kraus, *Editor*

SEMIOTEXT(E) · FOREIGN AGENTS SERIES
Sylvère Lotringer, *Editor*